SECOND CHANCES

JILL SANDERS

GRAYTON

SECOND CHANCES

DIGITAL ISBN: 978-1-945100-29-1

PRINT ISBN: 9798718417371

SUMMARY

Olivia has sworn off men for good this time. Having dealt with her ex, she learned her lesson. The only good thing about the man was that he gave her Simona, her perfect daughter. Now, however, she has promised herself that there is no man sexy enough to persuade her to break her new life code. No more men. Period.

Todd's dark past hasn't dimmed his sense of humor one bit. When he's asked to come back to his hometown of Silver Cove to help out an old friend, he doesn't expect to bump into a six-year-old angel. Meeting Simona and her knockout mother has him believing that maybe he does deserve a second chance.

PROLOGUE

Oliva held her arm close to her side. Part of her mind wanted to believe that it wasn't broken, but in reality... she knew it must be. Her skin over the spot was colored, and her wrist and fingers were swollen to the point that she couldn't bend any of her knuckles.

How had she ended up here? How had she allowed a man to do this to her again and just walked away?

Maybe it was because the entire town knew Brock. Maybe it was the fact that everyone who knew him always described him as such a nice guy. After all, Brock knew every single person in Silver Cove. Not that that was hard—it was a small town and the locals stuck close.

She wasn't a true local. She'd met Brock a few years back and, after a whirlwind dating period of nine months, had accepted his proposal. Shortly after their wedding, she'd gotten pregnant with Simona, the only person in her life that she could truly count on to love her unconditionally.

The first time Brock had hit her, she'd packed her bags and tucked baby Simona into her carrier. She had been at the

"

door when Brock had talked her into staying. He'd sworn that it was due to stress and lack of sleep.

The next time he'd hit her, it had been the extra beer he'd drank when out with the guys. She soon lost track of the excuses but had somehow let him talk her into believing that Simona couldn't make it without her daddy and that she couldn't make it, financially or otherwise, without him.

She'd let him convince her that she was nothing without him. That she couldn't even tie her shoes if he wasn't around. That she'd get lost, living out on the streets, and wouldn't even be able to dress herself properly if it wasn't for him.

For the next three years, she'd believed every single word of his lies. Somehow, what he said had started defining her, as if his words magically became the truth.

She'd convinced herself that it wasn't really his fault. That his excuses—that she'd needed to be taught a lesson for her many transgressions, such as forgetting to pay the water bill, for example—were valid reasons for what he'd done.

What kind of mother was she that she'd allowed their water to be shut off? Reason had tried to surface in her mind and remind her that there hadn't been any money left in their joint account to pay the bill because Brock had gone out drinking and had used up the money earmarked for it.

This time it had been because she'd needed to fill in for a coworker, and he'd wanted to go out with his friends. It wasn't as if she'd planned to work, but he'd been angry that she hadn't turned her friend down. That she'd put him out.

But she wasn't thinking rationally. Not when her arm was throbbing, and his evil words kept playing over in her mind, somehow twisting the actual truth into his version of the truth.

She'd taken a psychology class back in college, before she'd dropped out of school to marry Brock, and had learned all about the illusory truth effect.

If you repeat a lie enough, people will think it's the truth. She had fallen victim to Brock's lies.

Her only saving grace, besides Simona, over the past three years had been working at Serenity's Attic, a boutique of sorts right in the downtown of the quaint town of Silver Cove, Maine.

At least going to work was something Brock always let her do, during normally scheduled hours, anyway. He even made sure that he was there to watch Simona when she had to work. But she knew that was only because it was the only source of income in the household after he lost his job on the fishing boat.

After that, he'd been hired at the Walmart a few towns over as a night stocker. That had worked out with her own schedule and, between the pair of them, they'd taken care of Simona.

Then one day, Brock had come to her and claimed that he was in love with Bethany, another night stocker at Walmart.

He'd filed for divorce so quickly that she and Simona had only had time to pack up one bag each before Bethany had moved into the one-bedroom apartment they lived in.

She had faced her biggest fears. She and Simona were homeless.

Thankfully, she had an amazing boss. Crystal Holley was one of the most caring women Olivia had ever known.

When she had caught her and Simona sleeping in her car in the back parking lot of the store, Crystal had jumped in and offered her a place to stay.

They had spent almost six months living with Crystal in her massive historical home, Holley Hall, before things had changed. First, Crystal had made her manager of the store, which came with a big pay raise and more responsibility. Then she'd found a cute apartment just down the street from the store with affordable rent, and she and Simona had moved in.

While she'd lived with Crystal, she'd counted on the woman for so much, as Brock was being a completely absent father. By the time she moved into the new apartment, however, Brock had broken things off with Bethany and desperately wanted to get back together with Olivia.

Since she'd had a taste of her freedom, she'd denied him but had allowed him to watch their daughter, believing it was the right thing to do. Brock had never been anything but an amazing father to Simona, and she just couldn't deny that her daughter loved the man.

For a year and half, Brock had shown them nothing but kindness, then slowly, without her even realizing it some-how, he'd snuck in the jabs once again. It had started small, with him grabbing her arms when he was angry or shoving her slightly.

She'd been so embarrassed about letting him do that to her again that she'd convinced herself that she wouldn't allow him to do it the next time. Then one day shortly after, Kayla Thomas, now Kayla Holley after marrying Crystal's nephew Rowan, had caught Brock grabbing her arm at the store when they'd been arguing over work schedules.

She'd been so embarrassed that she'd made a point for the next few months not to allow Brock to pick up or drop off Simona at the store.

Now here it was seven months later, and things had progressed to where they had been when they'd been married.

She shifted slightly behind the counter and winced when the pain made everything in the room spin. She wasn't even married to the man, yet she couldn't work up enough guts to stand up to him.

Biting her lip to fend off passing out, she held onto the

countertop with her good hand and willed her body to get back under her control.

When the bell ran signaling someone coming into the store, she tried to focus her eyes as she called out a greeting and stood.

Then once again, the store spun, and her world went black.

She woke with Rowan Holley kneeling over her, looking down at her wrist. Rowan was the town doctor and hunk, but he'd married Kayla a few months back and had been officially off her radar. Not that she had one. After Brock, she'd turned that thing off.

"Don't move," Rowan said to her in a calm voice. "I've called for an ambulance." He was frowning as he looked down at her arm. "Want to tell me what happened?"

She glanced down at her now bright-purple arm and shook her head quickly.

"I didn't think so. Crystal is on her way." He sighed.

She groaned. "Couldn't you just... put a sling on it or something?"

His frown somehow grew. "Olivia."

How long had she known Rowan? Almost five years now? She'd never seen the man look so worried or pissed.

"Not this time. I'm afraid you might have to have surgery," Rowan said.

She glanced down at her arm and saw what she'd been denying in her head. Her arm wasn't just broken, it was shattered.

"Now, want to tell me what happened?" Rowan asked, his tone darker and more forceful. Still, there was tenderness behind his eyes.

She closed her eyes, feeling the sting of tears. Tears she hadn't spilled in the past five years. Tears which now seeped from her eyes uncontrollably.

"Brock. He was angry that I was filling in for Kayla tonight," she admitted. "He wanted to go out with the guys." She'd filled in tonight for Kayla after her friend had gone into labor. Olivia had been excited to know that Kayla was giving birth to her and Rowan's first child together.

She heard Rowan sigh. "I stopped by the store on the way home from the hospital to tell you that Kayla and Willow are both doing fine, only to find you on the floor."

"Willow?" she asked, feeling as if her body was floating.

"Yes, Willow Lori Holley was born about four hours ago," Rowan said with a smile. "When I drove by, I saw the lights and wondered why you were still here."

"I just got here," she said, feeling groggy.

"Honey, it's just past midnight," he said softly. "You filled in for Kayla at five."

"No." She shook her head. "That can't be right."

"Just rest, the ambulance is almost here now," Rowan said softly. She closed her eyes and could hear the ambulance.

That had been it. When Olivia had woken in the hospital after getting a few pins in her wrist and saw her sweet daughter, Simona, being held by Crystal, tears streaming down her chubby cheeks, she was determined to make a change.

No matter what happened in her life now, she was never going to allow anyone to hurt her or her daughter ever again.

CHAPTER 1

Two years later…

Olivia stepped out on the sidewalk and smiled. The warm summer air hit her, making her realize that she may have forgotten to put on deodorant that morning. God, she hoped she hadn't. It was going to be a very long day. She couldn't afford to sweat through her blouse. Still, she could always purchase another bottle of her favorite lavender deodorant from the store.

It was one of the perks of working there, having access to all the goods. Some of the stuff really worked better than big-name brands. Even if they did cost double, Olivia knew that they were well worth the price.

But on her budget, she had to be careful not to spend too much of her paycheck on the things she loved. Even with the employee discount, she could easily overspend if she wasn't careful.

Pulling the heavy rack of sundresses out onto the sidewalk, she took a moment to just breathe summer in.

The main street of downtown Silver Cove was abuzz with tourists already at this time of the day. Early morning was normally slow, since most of the out-of-towners were enjoying baked goods or home-cooked meals at one of the various diners, or just sleeping in at their rentals.

The streets were lined with brightly colored flowers that hung from the old-fashioned streetlamp posts or filled wooden and metal flower boxes on each street corner and shop window. They were replaced once a month by a local group of older women in town that was hired by the city. Each month the flowers were changed out with a new color, giving the town a new look. This month's color was purple, and the streets had never looked better.

At this point, she knew everyone in the small town of Silver Cove. Over nearly eight years, she'd made this her home, not just a place she'd been dragged to by her ex.

This was her place. Hers and Simona's. She'd found a small cottage on the bay last year and had saved up enough money to purchase her first home. She never would have believed that she could be a homeowner.

She could credit Crystal and the rest of the Holley family for helping her stand on her own and recover after the police had hauled Brock in for questioning.

He'd denied breaking her arm, but it had only taken a few hours for his hand marks to show up clearly on her skin. When she'd woken from surgery, she'd had a long discussion with Crystal and had finally admitted to what was going on. She'd been convinced to tell the police and officially press charges.

It had been the best day of her life. She had finally earned her freedom. Hers and Simona's. To this day, she hadn't looked back. Brock had gone to court and Olivia had had to stand in front of a judge and tell the woman about the years of abuse at her ex's hands. She'd been lucky that they were divorced, or so the lawyer Crystal had found her had said. That way there hadn't been a big messy divorce amongst all the other issues. She'd earned full custody of Simona that day, and Brock had been hauled off to the county jail with a five-year sentence.

She hadn't had the guts to look into his eyes as he was hauled out of the courtroom in cuffs. But she'd held her head up high and promised herself once again that she would never allow anyone to push her around ever again.

She hadn't expected to be as lonely as she was. Sure, she'd gone through a sexual hiatus when she'd still been married to Brock. Looking back at it, she was pretty sure it was due to the fact that he was getting it on the side with Bethany or whoever. Actually, when she thought about it, she was thankful Brock hadn't touched her back then.

Now, however, all these years later, she was beginning to realize that she didn't know how much longer she wanted to be alone. Letting someone in her life could mean going against her new life code, but there were ways around that. If she could find someone who just wanted sex without a commitment... But could she do that? Was she that kind of woman?

She didn't want to bring anyone around her daughter that she didn't trust, and trust came with a relationship. Right?

"Hard at work, I see." Kayla stopped directly in front of her, pulling her out of her thoughts. She hadn't realized she'd been standing on the sidewalk, staring, unseeing, at the busy street.

Kayla was pushing a stroller with two-year-old Willow fast asleep inside and Blue, their small rat terrier dog, snuggling up against the blonde-haired child.

"You caught me daydreaming," Olivia admitted. "It's so nice out here."

"It's why we decided to take a walk this morning," Kayla answered with a smile.

"I hate to tattle, but both of your walking partners are fast asleep on you." Olivia smiled down at the sleeping duo.

"Oh good." Kayla sighed. "Willow was up early this morning, and I swear she only got a few hours of sleep last night. She's going to go into preschool next year."

"Scary." Olivia shook her head.

"I know. CJ's first day of school, I was a wreck. I don't know what I'm going to do without my little Willow around for a few hours," Kayla admitted.

"Sleep," Olivia suggested with a smile. In the past few years, she and Kayla had become close. Closer than she had with anyone else. Maybe it was because the two of them had a lot in common.

They both had bad experiences with men in their past. Kayla's ex, the father of her son Connor James, or CJ, had been a complete douche to Kayla and had ended up killing himself shortly before Kayla and Rowan had married.

Where Kayla was now completely happy with a perfect family while married to one of the sexiest and nicest doctors in town, Olivia was still sleeping alone. Well, at least when Simona didn't climb in bed with her.

"I know, I just wish she would settle down to a normal schedule. I mean, she's two." Kayla sighed.

"A kid's schedule can be knocked off kilter so easily." Olivia remembered the struggles she'd had with Simona and smiled. "But she'll get back in the groove soon enough. You'll see."

"I'm just thankful for Crystal. I swear the woman has more energy that both Rowan and I." Kayla shifted and started rolling the stroller slightly.

Olivia laughed and then held the shop door open for a couple.

"Well, that's my cue. Talk to you later." She waved as Kayla took off down the sidewalk.

Olivia didn't mind her work. She actually loved it. It somehow leveled and settled her.

By the time lunch rolled around, she'd hit a lull with customers. She found that the best time to restock items was shortly after lunchtime. She could get a lot done without being interrupted.

Crystal would be there with Simona in less than three hours, and she wouldn't have time to do anything but help customers after her daughter arrived.

Normally, Simona would sit in Crystal's small office after school and either do her homework or watch her shows on the secondhand iPad she'd purchased last Christmas. But since today was the very last day of school, she had a few extra plans for her daughter.

Sarah Rothschild, Crystal's daughter, also known as Serenity, was going to pick Simona up for a playdate with her daughter Aurora.

The two girls were only a few months apart and the very bestest of friends, according to them.

Sarah and her husband, Ben, had another daughter, Luna, a few years younger, who trailed behind the friends and tried to keep up. The three of them always tried to convince everyone that they were sisters instead of just friends.

But Simona's jet-black hair, which matched her own, was in complete contrast to Aurora's and Luna's pale blonde hair. Still, it was cute that the girls loved each other that much.

After the girl's playdate, they were all going to meet down the street at Ed's Pizzeria for a big end-of-the-school-year party. Simona's first-grade graduation was the next evening, but Sarah and Ben were heading to New York the morning after graduation to visit his parents in the city, so they'd decided to celebrate tonight.

Since Olivia was still the store manager, she'd scheduled Cora to fill in for her that afternoon. The store wasn't big enough that it needed two employees working behind the counter at one time, except during holidays. Crystal and Daisy taught yoga classes at various times during the day in the large studio rooms in the back of the store. Lea, their part-time massage therapist, had clients coming and going during the daytime and had two small private rooms with showers for her clients.

But for the most part, the store made its money from the items stocked on its shelves. Items that most locals came in and purchased on a regular basis. Tourists would also drop a lot of money during the season, attracted by the store's eccentricity.

Serenity's Attic stood out from the other almost identical buildings on the street because of the bright blue-and-yellow sun and purple moon designs painted on the front of the building. The bright colors and designs covered every last inch of the storefront and marked it as an authentic hippie store. White lights hung on the eves, showcasing the place and all the colors at night. The front doors were painted bright purple with white stars covering every inch of them, a true testament to its owner's belief in astrology.

Not a week had gone by over the last seven years when Crystal hadn't read Olivia's star charts. Olivia didn't truly believe in the stuff, but it was interesting to hear it anyway.

This week's reading had her meeting her soulmate once and for all. Olivia didn't get too excited about that prospect, however, since in the past seven years, she'd had almost half a dozen of the same readings, all promising her soulmate was just around the corner.

This one, however, did cause her a moment of pause when Crystal mentioned that it was a child who would find her love. Olivia had tried to see what Crystal read in the cards. There were images on the front of each card, but how did she understand what they meant? After all these years, she had no idea what any of the cards meant. She remembered a handful of them, but each time, Crystal claimed they meant something different because of the other cards lying next to them.

As far as bosses went, Crystal Holley was by far the best one she'd ever had. It hadn't taken Olivia long to rise up in the ranks of the store. Crystal had been basically the only employee back when she'd applied for a job there, shortly after she and Brock had moved back to Silver Cove.

In a way, Crystal was the reason she and Simona had stayed in the small town. Her kindness had been one of the only lights in an otherwise very dark year.

Being freshly divorced hadn't affected her as much as being a single parent had. Brock may have been terrible to her, and she'd had to deal with his attitude and his control, but he'd been a father to Simona. Seeing her daughter go through father withdrawals had been hard. Simona had cried every night for a while, and Olivia had to comfort her as she cradled her daughter in her unbroken arm.

She hadn't wanted to tell her daughter how she'd hurt herself. After all, she didn't want Simona to get the idea that her father was a complete monster. She'd read enough children's health articles to understand what demonizing a parent could do to a child.

So instead, she'd lied to her daughter and told her that her father had to go away for a few years and that he loved her and would be back just as soon as he could. No one around her had wanted to break the mother code, so they had gone along with the ruse.

Olivia figured that she'd tell Simona when she was a little older and could understand what had happened a little better.

Then she'd had to juggle state-required counseling while dealing with a full-time job and a toddler whom she had to shuttle to and from day care each day. Crystal had made sure that she was paid enough to care for Simona and had even taken it upon herself to watch the young girl at times.

After a while, she'd fallen into a schedule and was thankful Kayla or Sarah had been available to fill in with Simona when she'd been unable to be there.

The three of them—four, if you counted Lilith Carriveau, Sarah's best friend—had formed a tight group, as they all had kids around the same age. Lilith and her husband Adam had three kids a little younger than Simona.

The entire gang was going to be there later to celebrate, one of many times she knew they'd get together over the summer. It made the second half of her workday drag out. She was really looking forward to spending the evening with her friends.

By the time Crystal showed up with Simona, she was so ready for the workday to be over.

Holding her little girl was one of the best feelings in the world. Her daughter was full of stories about her special playdate with her friends from the moment she ran into the store and wrapped her little arms around her neck.

For the next few minutes, she listened while Crystal helped a few customers. It was her shop, after all, and she loved it as much as Olivia did, if not more.

When the customers walked out, several bags filled with their purchases in hand, Crystal turned to her and asked, "So, are we ready to party?"

"I am, I am." Simona jumped up and down while waving her hands in the air.

Olivia laughed and swooped her daughter up into her arms, noticing how much bigger she'd gotten over the past few months.

When Cora showed up to take her place, she gathered her

daughter's many things and walked down the street to the pizzeria to meet their friends.

The place smelled wonderful and sounded like a playground. It appeared that every parent in town had the same idea they did. Kids of every age hung out at the old video games in the side room while their parents sat at the tables and cheerfully chatted and sipped their drinks.

They had a table in the back of the pizzeria where there was a little more room for the younger kids to play.

She had been really involved with a conversation with Sarah when she felt a presence hovering over her.

"I'm sorry to bother you," a rich deep voice sounded directly behind her, "but is this your daughter?"

CHAPTER 2

Todd O'Brien was home. How long had it been? Twenty years? It seemed like longer. Silver Cove had never looked so... good.

In the past two years alone, he'd lived through so much that the nightmares kept him up most nights. He didn't even want to think about the years before that, when he'd been in the service.

Still, all that was behind him now. For now, he was home. Even if it was an empty return and not the hero's welcome he'd once dreamed of. Instead, he'd returned to his childhood summer vacation home, which had been empty and boarded up for years.

The 1920s Cottage, as some people called it, had sat empty long before that fateful day when he'd gotten word overseas that his mother had finally given in to the cancer that had consumed her body bit by bit. The ugliness that had been hidden within the woman who had raised him had finally eaten her away and destroyed her physically.

She wouldn't be missed. Not by him. Not when he still bore the scars, both inside and out, from her years of abuse.

Helen Kelly had been born in Ireland to a simple farmer. Once she'd reached the age of consent, she'd married the first man who would jet her away from her boring country lifestyle, which happened to be Finnigan Walsh O'Brien, an older businessman who had swept in and purchased Helen's father's ranch and the rest of the ranches within ten miles.

Finnigan had been a wealthy real estate mogul, rich beyond even Helen's desires. But the man had also had a great kindness that would eventually be his undoing. Todd's father would end up trusting the wrong business partner, one who tried to steal all of Finnigan's hard-earned wealth and ended up killing him to spite his failed attempt. Helen and her young son, Todd, so named after Finnegan's younger brother, who had died of chicken pox when he was a small child, had escaped the night of horrors. But not unscathed.

Almost instantly, Helen had turned inward and grown bitter, leaving her young son on his own mentally. The wealth she'd dreamed of now consumed and twisted her. Instead of seeing the world as her enemy, her eyes had turned on her young son, a boy of the tender age of nine, who had just lost his entire world.

Ten years later, Todd walked away from the massive apartment in New York that he'd shared with his mother and joined the Army. And he never looked back. Even when he'd gotten word that his mother was sick, and hospital ridden, he hadn't sent word back to her.

Then again, he'd been living in his own personal hell at that point, and there'd been no time for him to deal with anything personal.

His first order of business after retiring from Special Operations Forces had been to open up and unboard the massive house, which overlooked the lighthouse on a small cape that held three other homes.

Upon hearing of his mother's death, he'd hired a lawyer

to oversee the selling of his family assets, excluding the summer cottage. There were more good memories in this particular home than there had been bad ones.

For the summers, they had traveled up to spend the entire vacation playing in the surf, boating, and fishing. That last summer, his father had tried to teach him how to water ski. They'd been happy here. In everything.

The first night inside the old place made him realize that he should have had someone watching out for the place all these years. At least he should have gotten it cleaned once a year.

The layer of dust on all of the furniture had taken a vacuum cleaner and two full days to clear away. There were boards on all the windows and doors, and he'd spent the following day removing them to get some light in the place, which had exposed even more dust.

Just when he thought he'd gotten the main rooms of the home clean enough to live in, he'd realized there were four bedrooms upstairs that he had yet to touch. He worked hard that entire first week to get the place livable before even stepping foot in town.

Since they'd only vacationed there, he figured that most people in Silver Cove wouldn't remember him. He remembered everything about the small town, though, right down to Ed's Pizzeria. It was one of the first stops he made, since he'd gone through the small supply of groceries he'd purchased on his drive into town.

He hadn't expected the pizzeria to be packed and had almost turned around to leave and find another place to eat. Then he'd smelled the pizza grease and his stomach had led him the rest of the way inside.

Thankfully, there was a small table near the front of the busy place, and he grabbed it before someone else took it. He assumed it would take a long time to get his beer and the large meat pizza, loaded down with extra mushrooms, that he'd ordered. He was happily surprised when his pie arrived within fifteen minutes. Even more happy when it was as good as he remembered.

He was so into his meal that, at first, the little raven-haired girl who was trying to open the heavy front door to the business didn't register. Then she stomped her foot in frustration when the door swung shut with her still inside.

Glancing around, he watched and waited for a parent to come to either stop her from leaving or help her open the door and walk out with her.

Neither of those things happened, and she finally got the door open. She stepped out on the sidewalk and started marching down the sidewalk, alone.

He didn't think twice. He was up and out the door, rushing after her, before he thought about it.

"Hi," he said when he finally caught up with her. The little girl glared up at him, but when she noticed he was an adult, she stopped walking. "Are you running away?" he asked.

"I hate him," she said, crossing her arms over her chest and stomping her foot again.

He held in a smile at the stubborn move.

"Who?" he asked, glancing around.

"Conner James." She drew out the name, and he held in a chuckle.

"Is he the reason you're running away?"

"I'm not running away." She rolled her eyes at him. "I'm going to my MeMa's house." She pointed to a large home less than a block away.

"By yourself?" He glanced back at the pizzeria, hoping her parents would come along soon.

"I'm old enough to." She raised her little chin in the air in a challenge. "Even if Conner James doesn't think so."

"Course you are, but maybe now that it's dark, it would

be best if you told your parents before you head out on your own. I'd hate for them to worry about where you went off to."

He could see her dark eyes dart back to the pizzeria, then she tucked her little bottom lip in between her teeth and winced slightly.

"Want me to walk you back?" He held out his hand for hers.

As if she realized what she was doing for the first time, she took a step back. "I'm not supposed to talk to strangers."

"And that is a great rule," he agreed. "My name is Todd."

Her eyes narrowed. "No, it's not. I know Todd. You're not him," she accused.

He smiled. "There could be more than one Todd out there."

She seemed to think about this for a moment. "Are there more Simonas?"

"Is that your name?" he asked. She nodded quickly. "Then, yes, I'm sure there are. What are your parents' names?"

She seemed to think about this. "Mommy."

He smiled. "See? How many other Mommies are there out there?"

She rolled her eyes. "Her name isn't Mommy, it's..." She seemed to think about it. "Olivia."

He nodded. "Simona and Olivia. I bet they are really common names just like Todd. How about we head back and find your mom? I bet she's real worried about you."

She squished up her mouth and then nodded and took his hand.

When they stepped in the door, his waitress walked over to him.

"I thought you'd skipped out on the bill," she said cheerfully. Since she'd been flirting with him earlier, he smiled.

"Just catching a runaway. Happen to know where Simona's mother Olivia is?" he asked.

The waitress knelt down and tapped Simona's nose. "Running off again?"

"Conner James is a jerk," Simona said with a sigh, causing the waitress to chuckle.

"Olivia is in the back." She motioned to a smaller area in the back of the pizzeria. "Jet-black hair, larger version of..." She rustled Simona's hair. "Can't miss her." She turned to go, then asked. "Want another beer?"

"No, thanks. But if you could box up the rest of my pie, I'll take it with me." He handed her a credit card. "Thanks."

"Sure thing." The woman turned and left.

"What do you say we go have a talk with your mom?" he asked Simona. He wanted to berate the woman for leaving her child alone for so long. Anything could have happened to the child. Over the past decade, he'd seen the horrors that man could do. Even to the innocent.

When he spotted the dark-haired woman sitting and listening to a blonde woman, he cleared his throat.

"I'm sorry to bother you, but is this your daughter?" He was still holding Simona's hand when the raven-haired woman turned around and assessed him with the most beautiful silver eyes he'd ever seen.

He actually felt his heart skip a beat as she looked at him. The waitress had been correct—Simona was a mini version of her mother. Except her mother was a knockout.

"Yes?" she asked, pulling her daughter into her lap.

He smiled, trying to seem very casual. "I followed her out to the sidewalk." Seeing the worried look flood those silver eyes, he held up his hands. "I saw her leaving the pizzeria on her own and got worried. Thankfully, I convinced her to return here. Where, I assured her, her parents would be worried about her."

Olivia turned to look down at Simona.

"Did you leave?" she asked

Simona was biting that bottom lip when she nodded. "Conner James says I'm a baby. That I'm too young to walk across the street on my own."

Another blonde woman sitting at the table jumped up, no doubt to go look for her son.

Olivia's eyes moved back up to him. "I'm so sorry," she started, but he chose that moment to open his mouth. He really should have thought about it before speaking.

"You really should keep a better eye on your kids," he blurted out. Those silver eyes went from soft and appreciative to hard and cold in a blink.

"Excuse me?" she said, shifting Simona on her lap.

"Simona could have been hit by a car or someone"—he motioned around to all the chaos surrounding them— "could have come along, and something worse could have happened."

"Thank you," she said, her tone now clipped. "I assure you that this won't happen again."

He narrowed his eyes at her and wished he could go back in time. Wish that he could stop himself from talking. But no, he just had to keep speaking.

"Maybe your husband could help you out and watch—"

"No husband. And as I said before, I assure you that it won't happen again. Now"—she stood up suddenly, shifting Simona onto her hip— "if you'll excuse—"

"Todd?" He glanced over at his name. The blonde woman who had been talking with Olivia and had been quietly watching him narrowed her eyes at him. "It is you." She smiled when he glanced her way. "I thought so at first, but..." She shook her head, sending her blonde hair flying. "It's Sarah..." She sighed. "Serenity."

He was pretty sure he swallowed his tongue and coughed.

"Serenity?" His first crush, first kiss, and first love. Then again, he'd been nine, so he really hadn't known what love was. "Wow." He hugged her back when she hugged him. He couldn't believe that she remembered him. She'd been his entire world that last summer they'd stayed at the cottage.

"I didn't know you were back in town." She stepped back and looked at him.

"Got back a few days ago," he admitted. "This yours?" He nodded to the little blonde girl sitting in a highchair, making a mess of her food.

Sarah smiled. "Yes, this is Luna and that"—she motioned to another blonde girl sitting on a man's lap— "is Aurora and my husband Ben."

Todd took a moment to shake the man's hand.

"Todd and his family used to come here every summer. They owned that place on the cape. The one we've been admiring for years," Sarah explained.

"The boarded up one?" Ben asked.

"It was boarded up until a few days ago." He smiled.

"Good to hear it. That place needs a little TLC," Ben said.

"I'll be giving it some over the coming months."

"Good to hear it." Ben bent over to stop his youngest daughter from spilling her drink.

"I'm sorry to hear about your mother," Sarah surprised him by saying.

"How did you…"

"My mother. She knows everything that goes on around here," Sarah answered. "Her husband is your lawyer."

He frowned and thought about it. "Your mom married Rory Sinclair?"

Sarah laughed. "She did. Almost two years ago now." She motioned to an empty chair. "Join us?"

Just then the waitress walked over and handed him his card and the bill to sign, then gave him his to-go box.

"Thanks, but I'd better…" His eyes moved back over to Olivia and Simona, who were watching him closely. No husband, she'd said. Single mother. The pull that he felt towards the dark-haired woman was something he normally wouldn't explore, but seeing Simona smile up at him had him sitting down.

"So, tell me everything you've been up to since I last saw you," Sarah asked.

He chuckled. "Since we were nine? You really want to know everything?"

She laughed. "CliffsNotes."

"Middle school, junior high, high school, Army Special Operations Forces, retirement, and now here." He leaned back in the chair. Sarah smiled, and a quick glance at Olivia assured him that she was listening and smiling as well. "You? Besides marriage and two kids?"

Sarah smiled. "Pretty much the same. Only instead of Army, I worked at my father's place."

"The resort. Right?" He remembered that Sarah's father had owned East Haven Resort, a swanky resort nestled on its own private island. Which is how he'd met Sarah in the first place. His parents had spent a great deal of time at that resort each summer, and he'd paid very close attention to a little blonde girl back then.

"A few years back, when my grandfather died, I inherited the place."

"You? You own the resort now?" he asked.

"We." She smiled at her husband, who was now holding the sleepy Luna in his arms. "And all of Elite International."

He stopped for a moment. The name was very familiar. Then he whistled. "I didn't know I was sitting at the table with some of the richest people in the state."

Sarah laughed. "We try not to be."

"How so?"

"My wife is very involved in charity work," Ben broke in. "Let's just say that she's put her family's money to work cleaning up this mess of a planet."

"Good to hear that." He glanced over at Olivia and smiled with he noticed Simona fast asleep in her mother's arms. "Looks like she left the party anyway."

Olivia glanced down at her daughter and smiled.

"You know, she told me that she was heading over to her grandmother's place." He frowned and tilted his head. "Which if I'm not mistaken was Holley Hall."

"She calls my mother her grandmother," Sarah explained. "Actually, most of these kids running around here think of my mother as their grandmother."

"Where is your mother?" he asked, glancing around.

"Oh, she and Rory are in London this week. They've been doing a lot of traveling. They're supposed to be back soon. She's going to love seeing you again," Sarah said.

He was a little overwhelmed at how much she remembered of him and his family. As if she'd read his mind, she laughed and said, "My mother and your mother were friends. They kept in contact over the years."

He tensed for a split second. He was sure that Sarah didn't sense it, but when his eyes locked with Olivia's, he could tell that she'd noticed. Something told him that when she was paying attention, she noticed everything.

"I wasn't really in contact with my mom after I joined the Army," he admitted.

"Which is why my mother's knowledge about you is vague." Sarah tilted her head. "So, you're back here for good or are you fixing the place up to sell?"

"I'm here for now." He hadn't really planned beyond getting the place ready and taking some time to himself. It wasn't as if he needed to go out and look for a job, thanks to his inheritance.

"Well, if you need a hand up at the place," Ben chimed in, "let me know. I can have a crew of workers over there for the cost of a case of beer."

Todd nodded. "I don't think there's anything that difficult that would require more than one set of hands. But I'll keep that in mind."

"You'd be surprised. We purchased a classic beauty a few years back and had to spend an entire year with renovations." He shook his head. "I was thankful for the help, and the beer, since I was so sore most nights I could barely move."

"Are you still working at the resort?" he asked Sarah.

"Yes and no. I hired my best friend Lilly to run the place," Sarah answered, motioning to another blonde woman sitting at the end of the table, trying to corral three young kids. "Then she went and had three kids on me. Now I've got Calvin Winters to watch the place."

"And your mother? Does she still own…"

"Serenity's Attic?" Sarah smiled. "Yes, actually, that's where Olivia and Kayla, work." She motioned to the other blonde woman who had come back with a boy of about eight years old in tow. Todd had no doubt that this was the famous Conner James that Simona had been talking about, because the boy looked like he'd had a stern talking to. He sat quietly at the table, watching the adults.

"So, what actually brings you to Silver Cove?" Olivia asked, gaining his attention. "I mean, do you have a job?"

"No," he answered. He knew he was being short but was curious to see how far in this line of questioning she'd go.

"Married?" she asked, her eyes scanning his hands.

"No." Again he remained vague.

"So, what? Your family owns a home here and you move in, with plans of fixing it up but not selling it? Without a job prospect?" she asked.

"Yup." He smiled. "That's about it." He shifted slightly, a

little uncomfortable talking about himself. After all, for the past ten years, he'd spent a lot of his time lying to others about who he was, what he did for a living.

He could tell instantly that Olivia wasn't satisfied with the answers he was giving. She bit her bottom lip, as if to stop herself from asking more questions. It was a move much like Simona had done, but on her it was sexy as hell. Her silver eyes assessed him closely while he ran his eyes over her.

She had a natural beauty about her. Anyone who looked at her would instantly be drawn in. Those full lips deserved as much attention as her sexy eyes.

While Olivia had been asking him questions, Sarah had pulled her youngest daughter into her lap. Now, she stood up.

"Well, it's way past these two little ones' bedtimes." Sarah shifted her sleepy daughter in her arms as she picked up a large bag from the floor. "It was nice catching up with you, Todd. I'm sure we'll be seeing you around town."

He stood up as well, taking his to-go box with him.

"Be sure to reach out to us if you need any help." Ben handed him a business card, which Todd tucked into the back pocket of his jeans before shaking the man's hand.

"Thanks, I'll keep it in mind." He watched the couple disappear and then turned back to the table. He had planned on just saying a quick goodbye, but then Simona surprised him by waking up in her mother's arms. The little girl took one look at him and then yelled his name and held out her arms for him. He couldn't help it, his heart completely melted seeing the little girl's sleepy silver eyes look up at him with complete trust and affection.

CHAPTER 3

For the past hour, Olivia had tried to peg Todd O'Brien. She prided herself on being able to read people. Maybe it had something to do with working retail or maybe she was just observant. Or maybe Crystal had rubbed off on her.

As he'd talked to Sarah, she'd listened to every word he said, and the ones he didn't. She'd picked up on his distress when Sarah had talked about his mother and instantly understood that, whatever had been between mother and son, he was not comfortable talking about it. She could totally understand.

She understood from his silence that he had enough money that he wasn't going to be out job hunting anytime soon. She itched to ask him some more questions, but since she'd just met the man, and one of the first things he'd done was berate her as a mother, she kept her mouth shut.

He was single, that much was obvious. He didn't have any kids of his own but liked kids, which might translate to wanting his own. Some men you could tell instantly that they didn't want to deal with kids. Brock had been like that initially. He had struggled with Simona at first. Their daughter had been almost two before he even took an interest in her.

Brock had made the excuse that he only liked kids when they were big enough that they could communicate what they wanted. Even then, Brock hadn't really known how to talk to Simona or any other kids he'd been around. He'd always seemed awkward and slightly annoyed.

Todd seemed genuinely happy to converse with her daughter. When Simona had opened her eyes, called out, and reached for Todd, he'd sat back down and let her sleepy daughter climb into his lap.

"You're still here," Simona had said with a yawn. "I thought you left."

"Nope, not yet. I got stuck talking to the boring adults."

Simona had giggled and reached up to touch his chin. "I like you. Will you come to my house and play with me sometime?"

Olivia gasped slightly. "Simona, you shouldn't invite someone you just met to our house."

Simona frowned over at her. "But he saved me. I was running away, and he talked me into coming back."

Olivia felt a little tired and overwhelmed by her daughter sometimes.

"We really should be going. You're going to have a big day tomorrow." She started gathering their things up.

"Tomorrow. Will you come to my graduation?" Her daughter said the word very slowly, as if making sure she said it correctly.

"Don't tell me you're already graduating high school?" Todd asked playfully, causing her daughter to go into another bout of giggles.

"No, first grade." Simona bounced up and down on Todd's knees.

Olivia saw Todd wince slightly and wondered about it, but then she was reaching for her daughter.

"Simona, I'm sure Todd is too busy to come to your graduation tomorrow." She shifted her bags and Simona then turned to Todd. "Thank you for convincing my daughter to not run away."

"Where and when is the graduation?" he surprised her by asking. She was so surprised by his question that Kayla had to jump in and answer for her.

"I'll try to make it, okay?" he said to Simona.

"Yippee." Her daughter started bouncing on her hips.

"Easy," she said, getting Simona to stop. "Now, why don't you thank Mr. O'Brien for helping you out tonight."

"Thank you, Todd." Simona smiled up at Todd and Olivia could have sworn Todd melted a little bit. He was falling for her kid. Who wouldn't? Simona was… a-freaking-mazing.

"You're welcome." He bent closer to her and tapped her daughter's nose lightly. "Promise me you won't go off on your own like that again." Simona sighed and rolled her eyes like she always did when she didn't want to own up to or agree to something. "I may not be there next time to help you out."

"I promise," Simona agreed finally. The fact that her daughter had a smile on her face when she did so concerned her slightly. She never agreed to anything she didn't want to do unless she was being bribed. Agreeing to not running off on her own again without any fuss? Yeah, she didn't trust her daughter. She'd been burned before.

"Thank you," she said to Todd.

"Any time." He nodded and picked up his pizza box, then turned to go.

Okay, so she may have watched him walk away. What woman wouldn't have? The man knew how to move. Especially in those jeans.

"That is one tall drink of yummy," Kendra said as she stopped to pick up the receipt he'd signed.

Kendra had at one point worked at the store with Olivia but had found that she rather enjoyed the tips at the pizzeria.

The woman was roughly her age, but she had way more game than Olivia could ever hope for. Maybe that's why she earned more at the pizzeria? She knew how to flirt. The last time Olivia had tried flirting with a man... it hadn't turned out so well.

Yeah, Todd was one tall drink that she'd like to enjoy. But this was real life, and she had far too many responsibilities to allow herself to dream about a man who had sexy brown eyes and a body she dreamed of getting her hands on.

Halfway home, Simona started nagging her that she had to use the bathroom. By the time she pulled into the driveway of their little home, her daughter was crying big crocodile tears.

Rushing her inside, she helped her daughter and then went back outside to gather up their items and bring them inside. Simona had changed from her party outfit to her pajamas already.

"Are you forgetting it's bath night?" she asked her daughter.

"Aw, mom." Simona's standard complaint caused her to sigh. "How about tomorrow morning I take a shower?"

Just looking down into her baby's silver eyes had her heart melting. Then her daughter pulled out the big guns and pushed out her bottom lip and put on a sad face.

"Fine." Olivia rolled her eyes. "But I better not hear a complaint tomorrow. Not a single one." She bent down and wrapped her arms around her daughter as she locked eyes with her. "Promise?" Simona reluctantly agreed by nodding her head.

The next morning it took all of Olivia's strength to lift

her daughter's dead-weight sleepy body and carry her into the shower with her. Setting her on the shower seat, she allowed her daughter to slowly wake while she did her own morning ritual before helping Simona wash her long black hair.

She was thankful that it didn't take much to care for the girl's hair, since most mornings they ran late, thanks to Simona's aversion to early hours.

Thankfully, her daughter kept up her end of the bargain and showered peacefully. But that was the extent of Simona's cooperation. It took twice as long as usual to get her daughter dressed, her wet hair combed and braided, and both of them out the door.

They were running more than ten minutes late to drop her off at Kayla's for day care. She'd pick her up for the graduation later that evening. Olivia was due to open up the store and planned on working until just after one.

It was so nice to have friends that could help her out with Simona and who had kids that her daughter liked to play with. Lately, she'd been complaining about CJ teasing her, but Olivia figured it came with the territory since the kids were around each other all of the time and CJ was at an age where having a little girl trail behind you just wasn't cool.

She and Kayla had talked in great detail about how CJ was changing and wanting to hang out with boys his own age rather than his little sister and Simona.

They'd determined to separate the kids' playtime by having some of CJ's other friends over each day. Kayla had decided a few months back that she needed to open a day care of sorts. It had turned from a joke into reality as the summer drew closer and several of their friends' day care options ran out.

Today was Simona's very first official day at Kayla's day

care. Kayla had eight kids signed up, not including her own two.

Olivia wasn't nervous about leaving Simona there for a few hours. After all, she and Kayla had been each other's backup babysitters for a few years now.

It was one of the reasons she had grown to love Silver Cove. So many people had stepped up to help her after Brock had been sent to prison. There hadn't been a moment since then that she hadn't felt loved and accepted. Which was new to her, as her own parents had shunned her years ago, long before Brock had come into her life.

They'd never been good parents, but kicking her out a week after her eighteenth birthday had given them the ultimate 'good parents' award. But they were old news.

Crystal and Rory had stepped into the role of Simona's grandparents seamlessly. Simona even called them MeMa and G-pa, names Simona had chosen for them. Her daughter did have a way of making others feel comfortable and loved.

By the time she unlocked the store, she was almost ten minutes late. She hated being late. Especially when it was her job to unlock the store and let the other employees inside. Lea was waiting for her along with her first client of the day.

Normally Crystal or Daisy would have been there to unlock the door, but Crystal wasn't due back in town until later that morning, and Daisy appeared to also be running late.

There was a small line of yoga class attendees standing out front.

"Sorry," she said as she pushed the doors opened, walked in, and flipped on the lights.

Many of the people mumbled their hellos or good mornings as they passed by, heading to the back rooms.

She locked her purse up in Crystal's office and got right to work setting the displays out on the sidewalk and rearranging some products that had gotten knocked down or put in the wrong locations.

More people shuffled in for the yoga classes, and she greeted each of them.

It wasn't as if early mornings were high sales traffic times. Although, since it was officially summer, she knew the tourists would start coming in waves each day, which meant more work for her and the four other employees underneath her.

Since Kayla had officially stepped aside to start her day care, she'd hired three more part-time employees, Amy, Jodi, and Tara to help with the shifts. Then there was Cora, who had been around almost as long as Olivia had and usually worked the night shift and closed up since she didn't have kids.

She'd just finished training all of the new hires and was positive that the store was in good hands for the influx of patrons that would soon be streaming through the doors.

Each summer was different, but also the same. There were days when they were so busy that she hardly had time for lunch breaks, and then there were days she sat and caught up on her reading between customers.

Today, unfortunately, wasn't one of those days. After the regular crowd shuffled in and started their first yoga class, the bell above the door never stopped ringing as customers came and went.

She even worked up a little sweat as she helped people find what they were looking for. Thankfully, she had just enough time to eat an apple behind the counter, taking bites between checking out customers.

When a group of young teens came in looking for summer dresses, she helped them each find the right sizes as they tried everything on.

She was standing up on a stepladder, using the metal

hook to reach a different size dress, when she heard that sexy voice directly behind her.

"Should you be doing that?" he asked, almost sending her toppling over.

She let out a squeal that sounded like something Simona would have done and gripped the handle on the ladder so she wouldn't fall over.

"Don't do that," she hissed as she glared over her shoulder down at Todd. He was smiling a very sexy smile back up at her, no doubt pleased with her reaction. Turning slightly, she frowned down at him. "What would you have done if I'd fallen?" she asked.

His smile grew. "I would have caught you."

Her eyes ran over him, and suddenly she imagined herself behind held by him, his muscular arms wrapped around her, pulling her closer. Then her eyes moved down to his lips, and her mind changed gears to imagine what it would be like to kiss him.

She just knew that he was a good kisser. Not like Brock had been. Oh, at first, she'd been too enamored with him to see his faults, a mistake she wasn't going to make again anytime soon. That thought had her clearing her mind and refocusing.

Turning, she took the dress down and stepped off the ladder to hand it to the young woman who was waiting in the dressing area.

Then she turned back to Todd.

"Is there anything in particular I can help you with?"

He was still smiling at her as if he knew what she'd been thinking moments before.

"I just stopped by to see if this place is as I remembered it."

"Well?"

He chuckled. "Yes. With some notable improvements."

She took the hint that he was talking about her.

"While you're here, you may want to look at some..." Then something terrible happened. She drew a complete blank as to anything they sold in the store. She quickly glanced around and blurted out the first item she saw. "Oils." That wouldn't have been too terrible if she hadn't pointed to the line of sensual oils Crystal swore by. Olivia felt her face heat.

Over the years, she'd sold a ton of those products and a few others along those lines without batting an eye. But now, here, with this man standing so close to her, hovering over her with his manly muscles and sexy looks, she blushed like a schoolgirl, which had his smile growing.

"Oh?" He walked over and took up the bottle labeled Handi Hand Job, and she closed her eyes as once again her imagination spun to an image of him running his oiled hands over himself slowly.

Damn. She was in serious trouble.

Swallowing her embarrassment, she stepped forward and put on her salesman face.

"This product is infused with hemp to awaken and enhance both your pleasure and hers." She picked up another bottle labeled Orange Creamsicle. "This is basically the same thing without the hemp. If you don't go for that sort of thing."

He turned slightly towards her, the bottle still in his hands. "Do you?"

"Pardon?" she asked, setting the bottle back down.

"Go for this sort of thing?" He waved the bottle in her direction.

Thankfully, she was saved from answering him when the group of girls came out of the dressing area, and she had to ring up their purchases. She knew every single one of them, as they were locals and had been coming into the shop for years. She'd overheard that they were all heading to the beach and had decided to stop in and get new sundresses for the trip. She wished them all fun and told them to drive safely. As they walked out, she realized Todd was still in the store, walking around slowly, looking at other items. Luckily, not the sensual oils and the various toys they had in boxes near the back corner. Most of the items in the store were not sensual.

"Find anything you can't live without?" she asked lightly as she stopped next to him. His eyes ran over her, and she could tell she'd pushed the sales pitch a little too far. "Are you getting settled in your place?" she asked, not giving him a chance to answer her first question.

"It's getting there." He nodded. "Crystal opened up a massage and yoga studio?" He motioned to the flyer he held in his hands.

"Yes, classes run daily."

"Have you taken any classes yourself?"

"Sure, I take the early morning classes on Tuesdays, Thursday, and Sundays. Are you thinking of taking yoga?"

He tilted his head and ran his eyes over her. "Maybe. I guess it depends."

"On?" she asked when he didn't continue.

"Do I have to wear tights?" he asked, causing her to smile.

"You're free to wear whatever you want. Some men wear gym shorts. Others wear those." She motioned to a rack filled with men's yoga pants.

He walked over and took a pair of bright rainbow yoga pants from the rack. "Not really my style." He held them up.

"They come in different colors." She pulled out a pair of black ones. "Something tells me you'd be more comfortable in black." She held them up for him.

"I do have a couple pair of gym shorts." He set the yoga

pants back on the rack then leaned on it. "So, don't you have a graduation to go to?"

She smiled and glanced at her watch. "I have a couple hours before it starts."

"What about after?" he asked.

"After?" She felt her heart skip a beat. Was he going to ask her out? If so, what would she say? Did she want to go out with him?

Her mind raced over everything she knew about Todd O'Brien. Nothing in her minute knowledge of the man screamed stalker, wife beater, or psycho. But then again, nothing in the first few months of knowing Brock had screamed any of those thing either.

"After? I take my daughter home and we watch *Frozen* for the millionth time," she answered easily.

"I mean after. Is Simona in summer classes?" he asked.

Her eyes narrowed. "Why?"

He shrugged. "I guess I'm just not too sure what happens to kids during the summer months anymore. I mean, from what I remember of summers…" He shook his head. "Most of the time I was left to my own devices for far too long. After we stopped coming up here, anyway."

"So, you used to spend your summers in Silver Cove?" she asked.

"Yes, until the summer after I turned nine."

"What happened then?"

"My father was killed." A look crossed his eyes and, for the first time since she'd met him, he looked… lost and sad.

She reached out her hand and touched his arm. "I'm sorry. I can tell that he meant a lot to you."

He seemed to tense slightly but then nodded towards the front. "So, is there a night you aren't watching *Frozen* with an eight-year-old?"

"Simona's six. She turns seven next month. Most nights, it's just me, Simona, and Elsa and Anna."

"Don't forget Olaf," he supplied.

She frowned at him. "How do you know about *Frozen*? You are single and without children, right?"

He chuckled. "Single, no kids. But that doesn't mean I can't enjoy a good flick."

"Something is wrong with you." She shook her head, causing him to laugh.

"If it eases your mind, I was forced to watch it overseas with the rest of my platoon." He shrugged. "It was either that or an old Bob Hope movie, and since some of the troops had kids and wanted to be able to talk to their daughters on video chat about the movie, Elsa won out."

She smiled and nodded. "I suppose I never really thought how hard it must be for our military men and women to keep up with all of their family's needs. If I wasn't able to talk to Simona about *Frozen* and her other favorite movies, she'd be upset. Once I made the mistake of forgetting Kristoff's reindeer's name. You would have thought that I'd just told her that all dogs don't go to heaven."

He chuckled and shook his head. "Forgetting Sven's name is almost a rookie mistake."

She leaned on the shelf next to him and crossed her arms over her chest. "Just how many times did you watch the movie?"

"I stopped before it became annoying. If you know what I mean."

"I do." She rolled her eyes. "How many times can a six-year-old watch the same four movies in her lifetime?"

"Let's see, take the number that she's watched it up to now, then triple that number each year from now until she turns twelve. I figure that's when girls stop watching cartoons and start chasing boys."

She laughed. "Great, now I have that to look forward to." She sighed and shook her head. "I think I was just past sixteen when I noticed boys for the first time."

"Oh?" He looked at her as if he couldn't believe what she was saying. "Something tells me the boys noticed you right away. I know I would have."

She laughed. "Something tells me you were too busy chasing every woman you could to notice a skinny, awkward girl like me."

"I'm noticing now," he said smoothly.

CHAPTER 4

Todd knew he was pushing his luck. He didn't want to come off as desperate nor did he want to appear like he was stalking Olivia. The fact was, he'd felt something towards her last night. Something he wanted to explore. He'd felt an instant pull that he hadn't felt in years, one he could afford to explore now.

Not that he hadn't been free to enjoy himself over the years, but when you had to hide what you did for a living from everyone close to you, it tended to put a damper on any sort of permanent relationship.

In the past ten years, the longest relationship he'd had lasted all of six months. Before she'd tried to kill him.

Kimber had been an assignment. After she'd found out that he was only using her to get close to her father, a diplomat under investigation, she had ended things abruptly. Abruptly enough that he'd spent weeks in the hospital recovering.

Being in Special Operations Forces is all he'd known for almost a decade. He was finding it difficult to acclimate back into the real world. A world where he didn't have to lie or try and find answers.

Yet, looking at Olivia now as she assessed him carefully, he figured he was still looking for answers. Just for a different reason.

"Maybe I'll let you keep looking," she finally answered him, making him smile. He liked strong women, enjoyed how the confidence oozed from her. "And maybe I'll hint that I have this Thursday night free. Simona's got a sleepover with some friends."

"Thursday is good for me," he replied, causing her eyebrows to shoot up. He understood that she was expecting him to officially ask her out. Old-fashioned. He liked that about her too. "What do you say we spend the time together? Maybe grab some food? You can catch me up on how things are around Silver Cove."

"I can do that," she said calmly. "How about you pick me up here around six?"

"I'd like that." He reached over and took her hand in his, making sure to let his touch linger. "I'll see you then."

She nodded and he turned to go, but he stopped when he spotted the organic food section and turned back to her.

"You sell local meats here?"

She blinked a few times and then moved back to his side. "Yes, local meats, dairy, honey, breads, you name it." She walked over to a large refrigerator that he'd been too busy to notice while admiring and flirting with Olivia. "All organic and humanely raised animals." She motioned around a larger section of the store. "It's one of the reasons we stay opened year-round. Locals help support one another."

He walked over and picked up a small basket. "I didn't think I was going to find anything in here that I wanted." He put a carton of eggs, some cheese, and a loaf of bread into the basket. He glanced over at her. "Besides a date with you."

She smiled. "Serenity's Attic has it all. We even have local soaps, shampoos, and other items. There's a farmer just outside of town that makes these wonderful cleaning products." She showed him the section that housed the McCall's products. "Everything from soap to wood cleaner. They're all natural and work great. I'll never use another glass cleaner in my life."

He thought about all the cleaning he still had to do at the house, windows included, and glanced down at his basket.

"I'm going to need a bigger basket," he admitted, causing her to laugh.

It took him two trips out to his car to carry in everything he'd purchased. Most of the items in the reusable bags that he'd purchased were cleaning supplies. The rest were groceries he'd needed to stock the place. He had planned on hitting the local grocery store after he'd visited with Olivia, but she'd had everything he wanted or needed at the store, saving him a trip.

Part of him wanted to get right to work cleaning the place after he arrived home, but he'd made a promise to a little girl that he wasn't about to break. He hadn't let on to Olivia that he'd be going to Simona's graduation because he didn't want her to try to talk him out of it.

After all, he'd just met them yesterday. But he knew that immersing himself in the community meant being active.

A very public event like a school's graduation could be a good start. Besides, Sarah's daughter was graduating as well, so it wouldn't appear as if he was just there for Olivia and Simona. Even if he was there to see Olivia again.

He'd been reminded about the graduation after seeing the flyer for it at the local hardware store earlier that morning when he'd stopped by to drop off a few window screens that needed repairing. He still had another hour before the event and spent that time cleaning as many windows in the place as he could.

He'd have to wait until he could climb up on the roof to clean the outside of the two rows of windows that faced the water. But he managed to finish cleaning every single window on the ground floor.

The cottage boasted more than three thousand square feet, six bedrooms, four baths, two original stone fireplaces, and a detached four-car garage, which included a second-story apartment.

Because of the uniqueness of the small point, which was home to eight other such cottages, the road to the two homes beyond his place cut directly between the cottage and the garage. The apartment above the garage included a bedroom and bath, a small kitchen, and its very own stone fireplace. His father had used it as an office when they'd spent summers there. So far, Todd had yet to climb the stairs to take a look at what sort of shape it was in.

Both buildings sat directly on the edge of the dark rocky man-made sea walls and had amazing views from every window. From the house, Silver Cove and the lighthouse beyond were visible from every west-facing window.

On the east side of the house sat the Atlantic Ocean. The entire point had stone or brick seawalls, which kept the water almost ten feet below the properties.

There was a good-sized yard area between the main home and the road, which had a tall hedge for privacy that needed trimming. Most of the yard was on either side of the home, and there was a small deck just outside the kitchen doors that he planned to expand. Off the back of the house, a large cement patio abutted the seawall, with its own low stone wall for safety.

You really couldn't beat the views from either patio. Part of him couldn't wait until winter, since he'd only ever visited the cottage during summer months. He desperately wished to see what it was like sitting inside and watching the snow fall over the water.

Still, three thousand square feet was a big space for one person to clean. He figured it would take another week or so before the smell of dust cleared out. Which is why he had needed the new screens and the windows to be cleaned. Some of them were so old, he'd needed a hammer to open them.

He left everything open when he headed to the graduation. On the way, he stopped off at the flower shop and purchased two small bouquets of flowers, one for Sarah's daughter and one for Simona. He figured it was the friend thing to do.

When he stepped into the gymnasium at the grade school, he felt a little overwhelmed and instantly wanted to back out and go home.

Then Sarah spotted him and waved him over to a small group of parents she was gathered with. It was too late to back away. He felt silly holding the flowers for the girls as he approached them. No other parents had gifts or flowers for the kids.

"I'm so glad you decided to come." Sarah gave him a sideways hug, since she was holding her youngest in her arms. "Are these for Aurora and Simona?" she asked, motioning to the flowers.

"Yeah." He used his free hand to swipe through his hair, noticing that over the past three weeks it had grown longer. Not that he needed to keep it military short, but his last assignment had called for a shorter look.

Over the years, he'd gone from buzz cut to below his shoulders with a full beard just to fit in where he'd needed to. The style he had now was his favorite and the easiest to keep up.

"The girls are in the back getting ready to walk down the aisle. You're welcome to sit with us." She motioned to where her husband was sitting.

"You remember my cousin Rowan, Kayla's husband. The man sitting next to him is Adam Carriveau, Lilly's husband. They have three kids but they are too small to be in school yet." She leaned closer to him. "They're here for support." She glanced around the almost-empty gym. "When CJ graduated two years ago, I think there was a total of twenty people in here."

He scanned the room and realized that there were only a dozen more than that number now.

"There she is," Sarah broke in. She started waving frantically with her free hand. "Crystal."

He'd forgotten that Sarah called her mother that. He couldn't quite remember the story of why. When he turned around and saw Crystal Holley walking towards him, it was as if he had stepped back in time. The woman hadn't changed a bit. Seriously.

She still had her long blonde locks, which were now in a sloppy braid lying over her shoulder. Her long flowing tie-dyed sundress could have easily been the same one she'd worn the last time he'd seen her, twenty years ago.

He watched recognition cross Crystal's face and then a large smile made the woman almost glow as she rushed over to engulf him a warm hug.

"I knew you'd be back," she said into his ear. "It was in the cards."

He'd forgotten that she was seriously into the gypsy things. He should have remembered after walking around her store.

"Or the fact that I mentioned it to you earlier today," Sarah added dryly. Crystal laughed and waved her daughter away. "You'll sit with us?"

"Sure." He didn't have a chance to deny her, because she'd taken his hand and strolled with him towards where Rowan and Adam were sitting.

Before he sat down, he turned and shook Rory's hand.

"It's nice to finally meet you face-to-face," Rory said quickly. Then the lights dimmed and the entire room grew quiet, and he got shushed. He sat down between Crystal and Sarah. A few moments later, Olivia rushed in looking a little frazzled. When she spotted him sitting between Crystal and Sarah, she stopped and looked around before finding an empty seat a few chairs down from him.

He was consciously aware of her the entire time. The music started, and a teacher welcomed everyone.

He'd never been to a first-grade graduation before, so he didn't have any expectations. If he had, this graduation would have blown it out of the water.

There was singing, dancing, puppets, and, yes, a dozen kids dressed in small blue robes with little caps walked down the aisle and graduated.

He couldn't help it—when everyone else stood and clapped, he jumped to his feet and followed along, pride for the kids he didn't know swelling inside him.

Maybe he was overreacting because his mother had never been proud of anything he'd done, or maybe he was finally free to show emotion. Either way, he enjoyed the moment.

When the event was over, everyone gathered around at the back of the room as they waited for the kids to gather up.

Olivia stood talking to Sarah while he chatted with Rory. It really was a small world, meeting the owner of Sinclair Financial Security Firm, which he'd hired a few years back to oversee all his financial needs after his mother's death.

Crystal turned to him. "A few of us are having a gathering at our place after. You're welcome to join us."

He thought about denying the invitation, but if he was

going to truly immerse himself in the town, he had to start somewhere.

"Sure. I suppose I can leave cleaning the rest of the windows until tomorrow." He shrugged.

Crystal smiled. "It's about time that place was enjoyed. I'm dying to see what your plans are for the place." She wrapped her arm in his and started walking out of the gym. He wouldn't have been able to get out of going even if he'd wanted to. Crystal was a very persuasive person.

An hour later, he stood in the dining room of her massive mansion. He'd never stepped foot in Holley Hall before, but since his return, he'd driven past it several times. After the first few moments in the three-story Colonial home, he understood from Rowan, Crystal's nephew and husband to Kayla, that the place was a historical landmark.

Crystal had given him a quick tour through the main floor, with its high archways, decorative molding, and dark cherry floors. The impressive twisted staircase led up to what he'd been told were several guest rooms. Crystal and Rory used the top floor for themselves, except for Rory's office, which was on the second floor.

He couldn't imagine having this much space all to himself. Then again, Crystal pointed out that there wasn't a day of the week that they weren't watching her grandkids.

From the way the kids hung on her and called her MeMa, he understood that all kids were hers.

"Sorry you were dragged along," Olivia said to him as he stood in the dining area, holding a cold beer.

"I'm not." He ran his eyes over her. "I'm enjoying myself."

She laughed. The soft sound caused his heart to warm.

"This"—she motioned around them—"can't be much fun for a single guy like you." She leaned closer to him. "You do realize it's a kids' party."

He wiggled his beer. "With adult beverages."

She laughed again. "I guess there are some perks."

He ran his eyes over her slowly, enjoying another perk of coming along. She knew instantly that he was assessing her, and she tilted her head slightly.

"Cake. Cake is a perk," she blurted out.

He held in a laugh. "I like cake," he said smoothly.

She took a deep breath and glanced around. "Did you meet everyone?"

He tore his eyes from her and glanced around. "Kayla." He motioned with his beer. "Rowan, their son CJ." He leaned closer and lowered his voice. "The bane of your daughter's existence." She chuckled and nodded. He glanced around. "Their daughter Willow is around here somewhere."

"In the kitchen with Crystal," she supplied.

"Right. Then there is Lilith and Adam, who is head chef at East Haven. Lilly, as she asks to be called, used to run the place but now plays mom to their three kids. Alex"—he motioned to a three-year-old napping on the sofa— "Brooke, who is two, and Emylia, who is three months old." He glanced around. "That's JT and Emma Wilder." He lowered his voice again. "Famous author and movie star, not that I gushed over either of them, thanks to ironclad restraint." She giggled again and he smiled, enjoying the sound very much. "Their twins, Sophia and Liam." He motioned to another man and woman, much younger than the rest and without any kids. "Calvin Winters, the new head of East Haven, and his new wife, Bella, who happens to be Ben's sister." He motioned to the two siblings, who were laughing about something one of the kids had said.

"Wow, you have a really great memory," she said before taking a sip of her wine.

"It helped with the job." He shrugged and watched her eyebrows lift.

"Job? What did you do in the…" He could tell that she was searching her memory. "Army?"

He nodded. "Special Operations Forces, Rangers" he said quickly. "This and that." He shrugged.

"Wow, I guess I just assumed…" She shook her head. "Rangers. That's like the elite team, right?"

He nodded again, not really wanting to talk about his past much. "So, I take it Simona's father isn't around much?"

Olivia glanced down into her wine glass. "He's not."

A look crossed her face, and he knew that just like his past, this area of her life was off limits. At least for now.

CHAPTER 5

There was no way for Todd to know just how much Olivia wished she could open up to him about her past. But this early in the game—and she knew it was a game—she wasn't going to spill all her dark secrets. Not since it was clear that he had some of his own.

Rangers? She was going to have to do a little more research on just what that meant. From what she knew, he was part of a top military group, the guys and gals that went in and did the jobs no one else could.

She looked over him again and wondered just how the job had changed him. She knew several other ex-military personnel. Some had PTSD, while a few others didn't.

From looking at how well Todd fit into the group of people gathered at Crystal's place, she somehow doubted he was affected much, but she knew that some people hid their pain very well.

"So," Todd said with a sigh, "Simona seems happy enough playing with CJ now." He motioned with his beer, and she glanced over to see her daughter being swung in circles by

CJ. Both kids were laughing and having a great time together.

"Yeah, they're like brother and sister at this point." She smiled.

"Really?" The tone in Todd's voice had her looking back at him.

"Yes." She frowned. "Why?"

"It's nothing. I just..." He stopped talking and started laughing, then motioned to where her daughter stood over CJ. Her little hands were balled into fists, and CJ was holding his left eye.

She thrust her wine glass at Todd and rushed over and pulled Simona off the bigger and older boy.

"What is going on?" she asked, trying to keep her voice quiet.

CJ stood up, still holding his eye, and said quickly. "It was my fault. I shouldn't have teased her."

Just then Kayla came into the room and, seeing her son holding his eye, rushed over to them.

"What happened?" Kayla knelt before her son and gently pulled his hand aside to expose a very bright red eye.

"I fell," CJ said, looking over to Simona, who was looking a little guilty and sad.

"Oh, well, let's go get some ice on that eye." Kayla took her son's hand and led him out of the room.

Olivia knelt before Simona and lowered her voice to a whisper.

"Did you hit him?" she asked. Seeing the guilt in her daughter's eyes, she sighed. "You need to go and apologize. Immediately."

"He said I laughed funny." Simona crossed her arms over her chest and stuck out her bottom lip, a move Olivia knew all too well.

The girl had obviously inherited her stubborn gene from her side of the family.

"I don't care what he said. It's never okay to hit someone else," she answered automatically.

"Well, now, that's not necessarily the truth," Todd said from directly behind her. Then he shocked her by kneeling down and talking softly to Simona. Instantly, Olivia wanted to correct him, to tell him to stay out of her parenting business, but he continued. "If someone bigger than you is picking on you or doing something bad, really bad to you, by all means, punch, kick, or scream at them and yell for help all you want." She understood what he was talking about now and let him continue. After all, as a parent, she'd had a few discussions about not talking to strangers or what to do if someone was hurting her. Obviously, her talks hadn't stuck, since Simona had bumped into a stranger last night and had let him drag her back to the pizzeria. Thankfully, back into her arms. But still... "But if someone is calling you names, especially someone you consider a friend..." He let that last word hang in the air. "Friends don't hit friends," he said softly, as he took her smaller hand in his. "Understand?"

Simona's eyes moved to hers as she nodded. "What about daddies? What happens when they hit mommies?"

Olivia tensed and kept her eyes glued to Simona.

"Sweetie," she said as tears started stinging her eyes. She'd believed her daughter to be too young to remember. How many times had Simona witnessed Brock hitting her? She'd tried very hard to shelter her from those moments. Obviously, she'd failed at that, as well.

"Well, then it's okay for you to tell someone, another grown-up. Someone who will get your mommy help. Like a teacher or another adult," he answered smoothly. "Why don't you head in and apologize to CJ. Since he already covered for you, I'm sure he's going to forgive you."

Simona nodded slightly and then sighed and looked over at her. "I'm sorry, Mommy," she said, and threw herself at her. Olivia hugged her daughter as a tear slipped down her cheek.

"I love you, baby," she said softly. She kissed her cheek. Simona turned and rushed from the room.

Todd stood up and held out his hand to help her stand up.

"It's not always as cut and dried as kids make things out to be," he said.

"Oh?"

"Sometimes there are other reasons behind someone's pain."

She watched his eyes turn dark, and she realized that maybe he had experienced more in his past than she'd first believed.

"You?" she asked.

He motioned towards the French doors that led out towards Crystal's garden area.

She walked over, opened the door, and stepped out into the warm summer evening with Todd at her back. She didn't stop until they reached the bench in the center of Crystal's little oasis.

"This is impressive," he said, looking around.

"You should see it in full daylight," she suggested as she sat down.

He walked over and sat next to her.

"After my father died, my mother… turned into someone else." He leaned back in the chair. "It wasn't necessarily the pinching, the slaps, or the pushes that hurt. It was the names, the verbal abuse, that stung the most." He sighed. "Mental abuse can last years; bruises fade in days."

She had never heard anyone else describe it so well. Then again, she'd never talked to anyone else about it. Everyone seemed so concerned about bringing it up around her that they remained silent.

"Sometimes the silence hurts as much as words," she said. She stilled when she realized she'd said it out loud.

"It's better to talk about it than to keep it bottled inside," he suggested. "I spent almost two years hiding from the truth."

"The truth?"

"About my mother. The first couple years I was in the Army, I kept everything bottled inside."

"What changed?"

"I met friends. People who had gone through similar childhoods." He reached over and took her hand in his. "The moment I was accepted into the Special Operations Forces, I took the chance and opened up to my team after a few of the others started talking in training. It was the best thing I ever did."

She thought about opening up to someone. Anyone. Just to let them know what she'd gone through, what Brock had done to her. The hell she'd lived in for years and had been too ashamed to admit, sometimes even to herself.

But the fact was, it was far too soon to open up to Todd.

"Thank you for talking to Simona," she said, changing the subject quickly. "I've had a few talks with her about stuff like that, but coming from you, I'll think she'll finally listen."

He smiled and dropped her hand. "I'd better get going." He stood up. "See you Thursday?"

She nodded and then watched him walk away. Part of her wanted to call him back, to tell him everything, this man that she'd only met yesterday. But she just watched him walk away, realizing she couldn't wait until Thursday.

When she walked into the kitchen, Simona was sitting on the counter next to CJ. The pair of them were laughing as they ate popsicles.

"Everything okay?" she asked, walking over to lean on the counter next to Kayla.

"Yes, Simona was just telling us how it's okay sometimes to hit, but not when it's your best friend." Kayla glanced at her, and Olivia understood that the kids had made up. She also understood the love in Kayla's eyes. Their kids had admitted that they were best friends.

For the next hour, the party raged on, as much as a party that included the young and the old alike could rage on. Kids ran around the house, ate sugar, ran some more, grew tired, and bugged their parents until finally everyone was shuffling out of the house.

Olivia carried a very sleepy Simona into the house and figured that she'd have to make at least two more rounds to the car to gather all the presents she'd been given, including Todd's flowers.

Simona had talked about them the entire ride home while holding them up to her face.

"These are my first ever flowers," she'd said several times. "Boys are supposed to give girls flowers, right?"

"Some boys do," she had said, glancing back at her daughter in the mirror, only to realize she'd fallen asleep with her face in the soft fragrant petals.

Olivia had to admit, she was sort of jealous. She'd never gotten flowers from a man. Ever.

Brock had never gone for that sort of thing and always brushed off anniversaries, birthdays, or holidays, claiming it was just a ploy to make businesses more money.

Since she worked for a business that paid her to make them money, she had tried to argue that it wasn't just a ploy, that it paid people like her a salary.

Still, when they'd ended up fighting over it, she'd dropped the subject and had never expected so much as a card for her birthday from him.

Her parents had never really taken joy in the day she'd been born. Nor any other day. She was what some called a second-thought child. After they'd had her, they'd had second thoughts.

From as long as she could remember, she'd raised herself. This, of course, had made her want to be out on her own. So, naturally, she'd taken up and run away with the first man who'd shown her attention. Out of the frying pan, into the fire.

She had to admit, though, now that Brock was out of the picture, life was looking nearly perfect. She was happier than she had ever been. She loved her job, her home, her child, and being a mother.

Okay, with the exception of one area in her life, everything was nearly perfect. Occasionally she grew lonely for adult physical activities. Not that Brock had been any good at it the last few years they'd been together. Actually, she could only remember the first few times with him being any good. After that, it was more… robotic.

An image of her and Todd wrapped in each other's arms flashed in her mind, causing her to smile. She might not trust a man for the long term, but that didn't mean she didn't want to enjoy them for the moment. And something told her that Todd would be very enjoyable.

She had muddled through her and Brock's relationship and the hell years of being with him for the sake of Simona. Brock had used her as glue to keep their relationship together.

She wasn't even sure that Brock really loved Simona. He had appeared to be a good father, but then again, he had appeared to be a good man too.

She didn't understand how anyone could not love their own child. Sure, she knew there were those out there like her own parents, but she just didn't have it in her.

Olivia loved everything about Simona. She loved the way her daughter smelled, talked, slept, ate, and laughed. Just being around her made her days brighter. If Olivia could, she'd spend every waking moment with her daughter.

She laid Simona on her pink comforter, slipped off her daughter's shoes and play clothes, and put on her favorite pair of pajamas before tucking her into bed. The first few years of parenting, she never would have let Simona go to bed without brushing her teeth or washing her face. Now, there was no way she was going to wake her sleeping daughter up for those trivial things. Hopefully, she'd still sleep in in the morning.

Six o'clock came early enough in the mornings. Sometimes, if she was lucky, she'd get a few minutes alone to herself to sit out on her back deck and watch the sunrise over the Atlantic Ocean. She didn't have waterfront property, but since the Millers had trimmed their trees a few months ago, she could just make out the gleam of water beyond their property.

She changed into her own sleeping clothes, glanced at herself in the mirror, and held in a chuckle.

"Okay, next time I go shopping for clothes, I need to purchase some sexy nightgowns." She smiled back at the image of the cat on her shirt.

She wasn't even a cat person. Not really. Simona had purchased the pajamas for her last Christmas.

Grabbing one of the new books she'd gotten from the library last weekend, she made herself some tea and climbed into her favorite chair to settle down and read until she grew tired.

When her phone chimed, she almost didn't read the text message. After all, no one ever sent her texts except Kayla or one of the other parents when they tried to coordinate their schedules.

-Hey Baby, I'm finally out.

Her entire body froze at seeing Brock's nickname for her. Could this be Brock? Was he out of prison? What the hell?

Her hands shook, and she started hyperventilating. He couldn't be out of prison this soon. He'd been given five years and it had only been two.

Why would he text her? Why would he act like nothing had happened? Was this some way of threatening her?

She tossed her book down and started pacing. Then she rushed around the house and made sure all of the doors and windows were locked.

Her phone chimed again with another message. The two words had the breath locked in her lungs and her heart racing.

-Found you

She knew she was being ridiculous because there was no way he knew where she lived. Not that the town was so big that she could hide in it, but… Had he found her house? Was that even possible? Oh god. Simona.

She rushed to her daughter's bedroom and glanced inside. She relaxed when she noticed her daughter happily sleeping, warm and safe in her bed.

She walked over to the window and double-checked the lock and closed the blinds. She desperately wished she could afford an alarm system. Or a dog.

She thought about texting the person back, claiming they had the wrong number. Or asking them who it was, saying she had a new phone. She could claim to be a man or someone different. So many ideas ran through her head.

When her phone chimed again, she turned it off and climbed into bed with Simona to try and get a few hours of sleep.

When Simona woke her, she was so happy and cheerful to

have the day off that Olivia almost forgot about the text message.

To celebrate, Olivia made chocolate-chip pancakes with extra bacon and two cups of coffee for herself. She'd only gotten a couple hours of sleep and needed the extra boost.

She turned her phone back on while Simona was watching cartoons and jumped as her phone chimed in her hands.

-Ignoring me Babe?

She shivered at Brock's nickname for her.

-Hello? I know you're there.

-Answer me.

-You fucking bitch, you'll pay for ignoring me.

-You think you can just do this to me? Lock me up? Take our daughter? Hide away? I'll find you.

Tears stung her eyes as her phone slipped from her fingers. How was she ever going to get through this? Was she ever going to escape this madman?

CHAPTER 6

aving a pipe break in an old house wasn't surprising and wouldn't normally have thrown him. But he'd been halfway through a shower that he'd desperately needed when it had happened, making the situation a whole lot worse.

He'd spent the entire first half of his day on the roof, cleaning each of the fourteen windows, and he'd removed an old bird's nest from the chimney area. That had led him to check out the other chimney, and he'd found a similar nest, this one wedged a little further down. When he'd climbed off the roof two hours after he'd gone up there, he was sweaty, covered in ash and soot, and hungry.

Since he'd run out of food again, he figured he'd head into town for a quick burger and then stop by the hardware store and then the grocery store once again.

He'd made several trips into town in the days since the graduation party. Each time, he'd hoped he would run into Olivia and Simona, but he'd had little luck so far.

He'd thought about their date tomorrow night and had

wished he'd gotten her phone number so he could text or call her.

He had run into Rowan at the hardware store, twice. Rowan was in the process of remodeling one of his bathrooms and joked about living in the hardware store and how the bathroom was trying to kill him.

Todd reminded him that he was the only doctor in town and didn't have the luxury of dying.

It had been nice to joke with someone and be asked to hang out sometime, after the bathroom renovation was done.

In the military, he'd been part of a bigger family. He'd missed that and had hoped that he would be able to find friends to watch a game or have a beer with.

But having only half a shower put him in a mood. Driving into town with his stomach growling, he pulled into the town's only burger place, Roy's Diner.

He walked in and took a seat at an empty table. Without looking at the menu, he ordered a burger and fries and an iced tea.

He knew the waitress was trying to be friendly to him, but he just wasn't in the mood for it and pulled out his phone to go over his checklists.

He was frowning down at a few messages he'd received about his retirement and health insurance when he felt a tug on his shirt.

"Todd?"

He glanced over and felt his heart kick in his chest. All of his anger, his weariness, and stress melted away when he saw Simona standing there, smiling up at him.

"Mommy said I shouldn't bother you cuz you look upset, but I just wanted to give this to you. I colored it." She held up a place mat, like the one in front of him on the table, only this one was brightly colored. It was perfect.

"Wow." He lifted her up easily and set her in his lap. "You did this?" He took the paper from her.

"Yes." She smiled at him.

"All by yourself?" he asked, his eyes scanning the diner for Olivia. Seeing her watching them from a booth near the back, he nodded his greeting to her.

"Mommy colored this part." Simona motioned to the small dog, which was colored brown, instead of the bright colors the rest of the child's menu was covered in.

"I like this part the best." He ran a finger over the purple house. "Is this your house?"

"No, our house is yellow." She giggled.

He smiled. "My house is boring gray."

"Want to come eat with us?" She pointed across the room. His eyes locked with Olivia's, and he understood immediately that it was okay with her, since she nodded. "We ordered and everything."

Todd chuckled and stood up, holding Simona in his arms and his iced tea in his free hand. When he walked by the waitress, he told her he was moving tables.

"Hi," Olivia said when he sat down, letting Simona sit next to him in the booth.

"Hi. This is a nice surprise," he admitted.

"You looked like you could use it." She shifted her head slightly. "Bad day?"

He sighed. "A pipe burst in the house and cut my shower short. I'm heading to the hardware store after lunch for what I need to fix it."

"Oh." She winced. "Sorry to hear that." She smiled. "I thought I smelled something."

He chuckled and for the first time since seeing the water rushing from the wall, he relaxed. "How have you two been?" He glanced down at Simona. "Now that you're a first-grade graduate, I bet you have all sorts of job offers."

Simona laughed and shook her head quickly side to side. "I'm only six." She rolled her eyes before she started coloring again, this time on his place mat.

"Is there a lot of work to do around your home?" Olivia asked.

"Not really. I mean, it's livable. Just not… updated. I'm actually thinking about doing some upgrades while I'm at it." He shrugged. "The kitchen could stand to be brought into this century."

"When we moved into our place, I had to update the bathrooms. I learned how to install tile myself."

He thought about the bathrooms and realized he wanted to remodel them as well.

"Okay, I might be calling you for help when I start work in the bathrooms." He thought about all the other things he wanted to update in the home. He was looking forward to starting some of the work since he enjoyed working with his hands. "The place has good bones; it's just been neglected for years and is seriously outdated."

"Are you going to do all the work yourself?" she asked.

"Whatever I can do." He nodded. "A lot of it isn't hard, just tedious."

"Like plumbing?" she asked with a chuckle.

"Yeah."

"Well, I have the name of a plumber, if you need," she offered.

He figured it was a perfect time to ask for her cell number. But just then, their food arrived, and they shifted discussion to her and Simona's summer plans.

They were halfway through the meal when he noticed that every single time the diner door opened, she glanced over with a worried look on her face.

"Expecting someone?" he asked casually as he glanced over his shoulder to watch a young couple walk in.

"No." She shook her head and averted her eyes from his. She sucked her bottom lip between her teeth, a sure sign of worry.

Glancing down at Simona, who was busy eating the pancakes he'd helped her cut into small bites, he lowered his voice.

"If I've interrupted your day…"

"No, it's nothing like that." Olivia sighed and glanced towards Simona, and he instantly got the hint that, whatever she was worried about, she didn't want her daughter to know about it.

"Maybe after we finish eating, we can take a short walk in the park?" he suggested.

Olivia thought for a moment and then nodded. "We'd like that," she said with a smile.

"Park!" Simona yelled jubilantly, gaining the attention of a few people around them, who either giggled or shook their heads in disappointment at the outburst.

"Simona, we've talked about this. Yelling in public is not okay," Olivia said quickly.

Simona covered her mouth and nodded. "Sorry, Mommy," she said through her fingers, but he noticed a slight giggle escape as well.

He tried not to smile, really, he did. But Simona was just so… fun.

After they finished eating, they headed out into the park and the sunshine. The playground was a hot spot today. More than a dozen kids ran around while their parents sat on the benches and watched or played with the kids themselves.

Since he wanted to see what was on Olivia's mind, they sat on a bench under a large tree while Simona played with one of her friends, who happened to be in the park.

As with the diner, she scanned the park, returning to her daughter often.

"Want to tell me what has a worried look in your eyes?" he asked.

She sighed slightly. "I received a few text messages the other night."

"From?"

"My ex."

"Is that a problem?" he asked, trying not to push her, since she'd made it clear that the topic was off limits.

"Two years ago, no, it wouldn't have been." She glanced down at her fingers. "But now…" She sighed.

"Where has this ex been for the past two years?"

"Jail," she answered quickly.

He tensed as his eyes flew to Simona, then around the park, to scan for danger.

"For?" he asked, turning back towards her.

Since her eyes were locked on Simona, she hadn't seen his worry.

"It's a long story."

"So, now you're worried since you're getting text messages from an ex," he said and she glanced at him and nodded. "One that is in jail?"

"The one that is supposed to be in jail for another three years. I found out that he was released on parole last week, thanks to good behavior," she answered dryly.

"And you let me take you to a park?" He started to get up, but she placed a hand on his.

"Todd, it's okay. I've been assured that he's not back in town and that he had to agree to a restraining order as part of his early release. He can't get near me."

He relaxed slightly, picking up on the small hints that it wasn't about Simona. That whatever her ex had done, it was about Olivia alone.

"Yet, you're still watching who walks in the door and who is in the park?" he asked.

She sighed and relaxed back. "Old habits. When he was first locked up, I jumped at shadows." She shrugged.

Since she was still touching his hand, he turned his wrist and locked fingers with her.

"If you two don't want to be alone, I could use some help out at the house?" he offered. "I can download *Frozen* for Simona, and you can help me do some plumbing?" he asked with a smile. He had no hope that she would take him up on her offer, since it was just meant to be a joke, but she surprised him by nodding.

"I think we can lend a hand. We might want to change first." She motioned towards Simona's dress.

"You know where I live." He squeezed her hand lightly. "I've got to hit the hardware store first anyway."

She smiled. "Thanks, I..." She shook her head. "I don't normally unload like this on strangers." He winced slightly and she smiled. "Men I have a scheduled first date with," she corrected, and he chuckled. "I guess you got me at a vulnerable time."

He lifted her hand and brushed his lips across her knuckles. "Then you can count lunch as our first date."

She smiled. "And this was our first kiss?" she teased.

His smile slipped slightly as he thought of brushing his lips across hers. What it would feel like. How she would respond to his touch. Something told him that she'd come alive. That she'd be more than anything he'd experienced before. He knew that he'd want to savor that moment.

"No." He shook his head. "Our first kiss will be far more private and far more... than this." He heard her breath hitch before he stood up, and he glanced towards Simona one last time to make sure the girl was safe. "I'll see you soon."

She nodded and he turned to walk away.

At the hardware store, he purchased the items he believed he'd need to make the repairs along with a coloring book and a box of crayons that he spotted at the checkout stand.

An hour later, he was covered in sweat and water from a new busted pipe in his shower area when his doorbell rang.

"Come in," he called out as he held his hand over the shooting water to keep it out of his face.

Since he hadn't had a chance to clean the upstairs of the house yet, he'd taken to sleeping in the only bedroom on the main floor. It was small, but still perfect enough for him. The bathroom in the hallway on the other hand, was the one giving him real problems.

He knew that if he couldn't get this bathroom fixed, there was no use trying one of the three upstairs.

"Todd?" Olivia called out.

"Back here," he replied, trying to get the wrench, which just happened to be out of his reach.

"Oh my!" Olivia said when she walked into the bathroom. Then she was beside him, a towel and the wrench in her hands.

He watched in amazement while she expertly turned a small red valve under the counter until the water stopped spraying in his face. He hadn't even seen the connection, let alone known what it was for.

"How'd you do that?" he asked, using the towel she handed him to wipe his face.

She chuckled. "After a year of living in an old house, I learned how to turn off the water." She smiled and sat on the edge of his tub as she looked at the damage.

"You saved my bacon." He sat down on the wet tile and leaned against the wall. "Where's Simona?"

"Here." The little girl appeared in his bathroom door. "This your house?"

"Yup." He smiled.

"You're all wet." She frowned over at him.

He laughed.

"There's a hole in your wall." Simona frowned as she leaned closer to look at the disaster that used to be his bathroom.

"Yup. But your mommy is here now, helping me fix it." He brushed a finger down her nose.

"Mommy fixed our broken toilet," she said and then leaned closer and lowered her voice. "I flushed a bear down it and water kept coming up. What did you flush down the toilet?"

He smiled. "Nothing. I think the pipes just aren't used to having water in them. The water has been off in this old house for years."

"Oh," Simona said, seeming to lose interest. "I have a movie." She held up a bag.

"Right." He hoisted himself up and then tossed the towel in the sink. "I'll show you how to work the television." He held out his hand, and she placed her little one in it and followed him out into the den.

After getting her set up, he walked back into his bedroom and pulled off his soaking shirt to put on a dry one.

When he turned around, Olivia was standing in the bathroom door, watching him, a smile curving her lips upwards.

"I wasn't expecting to get a show." She crossed her arms over her chest as she ran her eyes over his bare chest.

Hearing Simona sing along to the movie in the next room, he slowly walked towards Olivia and pulled her closer until her chest was up against his own.

She felt so good in his arms. How long had it been since he'd allowed himself to just let go and be with someone he wanted?

Her tongue darted out slowly and ran across her bottom

lip. A low groan built up and escaped him as his anticipation grew.

He waited, just a heartbeat, before dipping his head down and taking her mouth. She tasted better than he could ever remember anything tasting in his life. She was soft, warm, and fit perfectly against his own body.

Her arms wrapped around him, holding him close against herself. He could have sworn he felt her shiver, but it could have been his body shaking instead.

When he finally pulled away, they were both breathless, and he was more turned on than he'd been in years.

"I think we should..." He heard Simona laughing in the next room and took another step away from Olivia.

"Work on fixing your pipes." Olivia nodded. "Water pipes," she corrected as her face heated.

He chuckled as he grabbed a dry shirt and pulled it on over his head.

"May I just say, yum," she said.

He met her eyes. "You taste like cherries. I can't wait to get another sample, soon."

She swallowed and her eyes went dreamy, then she shook her head and nodded. "Work first."

"Yes," he agreed.

A half an hour later, he was more than impressed with Olivia's knowledge of plumbing and of electric work as well. She talked as she worked, and since it was obvious that she knew far more about the repairs that needed to be done than he did, he stood back and watched her.

"So, I guess watching too many home repair shows on television does pay off," she said over her shoulder.

"If you learned all this while watching TV, then I should be one of the best football and basketball players ever." He smiled.

She laughed. "Something tells me you're really good at

sports." She shifted so she could run her eyes over him. "With a body like that."

He smiled. "I like what I see too."

Just then Simona stepped into the bathroom. "I have to go potty."

Todd jumped up from his spot on the closed toilet lid. "I'll just..." He walked out the bathroom door and checked his phone. There were two messages. One was from Rory with an update on the sale of the rest of his mother's assets, and one was from a blocked number that simply said.

"Found you." Reading it, he felt his blood turn to ice.

CHAPTER 7

Something changed in Todd's behavior after Simona interrupted their flirtatious conversation. It had been years since she'd used her skills to lure a man into liking her. At least that's how she thought of it.

He'd been laughing and having a good time while he continued to try and help her fix the broken galvanized pipes. She had suggested that he get the rest of the old plumbing in the house checked out and replaced. He'd taken down the name and number of the plumber that had updated her house.

When he'd come back into the bathroom after Simona returned to watching her movie, he'd seemed… off. Distant. Worried somehow.

"Problems?" she asked him.

"Hm?" He sighed and shook his head. "Nothing that I can't handle." He turned and motioned to the wall. "Think she's going to hold up?"

"This one will, but like I said, you'll want to get the rest of the old pipes checked out. The electricity too." She reached up and tightened a light bulb that had gone out and smiled when it turned on after she screwed it in all the way. "What else can I help you with?"

"That was it for today." He leaned against the door frame.

Her mind flashed to the image of how sexy he'd looked shirtless earlier. She couldn't remember ever seeing a more perfect six pack and pecs, even at the gym she worked out at two times a week. The man was full of lean, toned muscles that she itched to explore.

"Want to show me around your home? I've been dying to see what one of these places on Widow Reed's Point looks like on the inside," she said.

"Widow Reed?" He shook his head. "I thought it was called Rocky Point?"

"Oh, it is." She smiled. "But a legend has the locals calling it Widow Reed's Point instead."

He smiled again. "Oh?" He motioned for her to step out of the bathroom. "While I show you around, why don't you tell me all about it."

For the next half hour, Todd walked both her and Simona around the massive six-bedroom home. There was the smaller bedroom downstairs, which Todd was currently using, and four larger bedrooms on the second floor, plus a massive master bedroom that sat on the third floor along with an equally large office. The master bedroom had four wide windows that overlooked the blue waters of the cove. She could just make out Silver Cove Harbor from that side of the house. The other side of the house, the one with the office, overlooked the darker waters of the Atlantic.

As they made their way through the older home, she told the story of the young bride back in early nineteen hundred who had fallen in love with a young captain in the navy. The young man had risked his life and that of his shipmates to save the entire town of Silver Cove by fighting off pirates and trying to lead them away from the newly formed town.

"The ship, Emma Bella, fought off two pirate ships for more than two days, until all three ships sank to the bottom of the cove one stormy night." She finished the story, one of her favorites about the town.

"Is this a playroom?" Simona asked, rushing over to stand next to an old wooden rocking horse.

They had just stepped into a long narrow room with multiple windows overlooking the fenced yard areas that sat on the sides of the home.

"This is my old schoolroom," Todd said as Simona rushed around the room, trying to sit in one of the two classic wood and iron school desks.

The room could have easily schooled a small group of kids. There was even an old black chalkboard hanging on one wall.

"Schoolroom?" she asked Todd.

"Yeah. We only came up here in the summers, but my father wanted me to be ahead in classes, so most summers I had tutors," he answered with a shrug.

"Kids should be able to be free during summers." She thought about Simona being stuck indoors all summer long.

"It wasn't that bad. Normally, I only spent an hour or two inside each day. Some of the classes I rather enjoyed. I had a French tutor…" His smile grew. "Miss Sonya. She was my favorite."

Olivia's eyebrows shot up. "Adam's grand-mère?" she asked.

He frowned. "Adam… Carriveau. I hadn't put it together." He laughed. "Yes, I suppose so." He nodded.

"She's still around. Last time Adam took us out on the boat, Miss Sonya tagged along. Simona's learning some French from her as well and loves her."

They both turned and watched Simona rush around the room as if it was the best thing in the world.

"She wants to be a teacher when she grows up," Olivia explained when her daughter started writing on the chalkboard.

"Well, she can come over here and play anytime she wants. I was going to turn this room into a home gym."

"Oh," she said. Thinking about turning the charming old schoolroom into a home gym made her heart sink slightly. But she figured he had the right to do whatever he wanted with his space. Besides, she did like the benefits of him working out.

"But then again, I still have the room above the garage I could use as a gym instead." He tilted his head. "Which would be better actually, since there's a small kitchen and bathroom over there."

"You have a garage with more rooms above it? Where?" she asked.

He walked over to a window and motioned. "The garage sits across the one-lane street. Because of the makeup of the point, most homes have their garages on the other side of the lane." He pointed to the four-car garage. Sure enough, there was a second story to the smaller building that matched the main home's design.

If this was his family's summer home, she wondered what kind of place he'd grown up in?

"Where did you live when you weren't here?" she asked.

"A brownstone in New York. My mother remained there after my father's death. It was the first place I sold after her death."

"First place?" she asked.

"All in all, they had five properties." He shrugged. "The brownstone was the first to go."

"Bad memories?" she asked softly.

"Too many. Besides, I could never really see myself settling in the city. As a kid, I spent my winter months dreaming of coming back here." He glanced around and she saw his eyes soften. Even though she'd first believed the room had been a summer prison for the young Todd, she now realized he'd been happy here.

She couldn't remember ever being that happy anywhere. She thought about her childhood home just outside of Chicago, which her parents still lived in. She'd never really seen herself staying in the city either. It was one of the reasons she'd remained in Silver Cove after the divorce. It had been everything she'd hoped for in a home. The small town was a perfect setting to raise Simona.

"When was the last time you visited here? I mean, after your father passed," she asked. Since Simona was enjoying herself, she sat down in one of the desks.

"I didn't," he admitted. "Until about a month ago, I hadn't stepped foot in Maine since I was nine."

"Yet you remember it fondly enough to move back here? What if you end up not liking it?"

He shrugged and sat in the other desk next to her. "I guess I'll fix the place up and sell it, then."

"Just like that?" she asked as she started wondering what she and Simona would do if they didn't live in Silver Cove. Where would they go? She couldn't think of any other place she wanted to be.

He shrugged. "In the past ten years, I've lived in a dozen different countries," he said casually.

She turned and watched Simona writing her name on the chalkboard, just like a teacher would have, and her heart sank at the thought of allowing her daughter to grow close to a man who wasn't committed to sticking around. She'd done that once before with Brock. She doubted Simona's heart could bear being broken again.

It was the reason she'd avoided dating in the past two years. She didn't want to be the reason her daughter got another broken heart. It had taken months for Simona to stop crying over Brock not returning for her. In the end, it had been the support that her friends had given them that allowed her to recover. They had kept Simona so busy and entertained that she'd stopped asking when Brock was going to come back for her.

"What about you?" Todd asked her, shaking her out of her thoughts.

"Me?" she asked.

"Have you always lived in Silver Cove?"

"Oh, um, no, I've been here for almost eight years. We moved back to Brock's hometown when we found out I was pregnant with Simona." She glanced over at her daughter who was now quietly reading a book in a corner filled with bookshelves and old books.

"Before that?" he asked.

"Chicago." She glanced over at him. "My parents still live just outside of the city."

"After the divorce, you stuck around here?" It was more of a question than a statement.

"Yes." She smiled. "I came into town for Brock and stayed for the people I'd grown fond of." She sighed. "I had a great job, an amazing boss, and people who helped me through a really rough time."

He reached over and took her hand gently. The same hand that had been shattered by the last man she'd trusted. Looking into his eyes, she somehow knew that Todd was nothing like Brock. The man sitting across from her was more responsible than Brock had ever been. Better looking by far. More muscular, kinder, and more patient with Simona. And that was just the few things she'd noticed about him so far.

"What sort of things did you do for the Special Operations Forces?" she asked. His face changed, somehow growing sadder and more distant. His hand dropped away from hers.

"Jobs that no one else could do. Covert missions in places I'm not allowed to admit to being." He shifted.

She'd heard about special teams of people who did some of the most dangerous jobs the military had to offer.

"I understand," she said suddenly. "You probably can't really talk about any of your experiences."

"The experiences yes, the details, no." He smiled.

"So, you just retired and moved here?"

"Yeah." He sighed. "I... there's..." He sighed again, this time more heavily. "A few of my team have been..." He shook his head and stood suddenly. "How about some dinner? I have some burgers and hot dogs?"

She got the hint that he didn't want to talk about his work. There were things she didn't want to verbalize either. Not yet, at any rate.

"Do you have chips?" Simona asked from across the room. "The wavy kind?"

He smiled and she watched him fully relax and change back into his old self. Even his smile was back as he stood up and walked over to where Simona was. "I do. I also have some cookies that you can have after we eat, if it's okay with your mom."

Simona, being her daughter, narrowed her eyes. "What kind of cookies?"

Todd laughed. "Chocolate chip. My favorite."

"Mine too." Simona jumped up and down and reached for Todd's hand.

She hadn't planned on staying around his place for that long, but as she sat out on the deck that overlooked the water and watched him grill burgers and hot dogs, she realized this was just what she needed. A relaxing time around a man she liked. She told herself it was good for Simona as well.

Her daughter needed good male role models in her life. Not that she didn't have any—there were all of the husbands of the women she was closest to in town. Men she admired as well as liked.

While they ate, they talked about her work and about all of the things he wanted to improve around the house. The downstairs of the home was cleaned and appeared to be where he was currently living, but the upstairs was still extremely dusty and most of the furniture was covered with large white cloths.

He explained that he hadn't had a chance to open up the rooms yet, nor did he think he wanted to until he was done with the main floor.

"It took me almost two days with a new lawnmower I had to purchase at the hardware store to clear out the yard." He motioned to the green patch of grass inside an old stone wall.

"I'm hoping the fertilizer and grass seed I put down will choke out all the weeds." He looked out over his yard.

"Are you going to be planting flowers in the beds?" she asked, looking at the long rows of flower beds against the fenced area.

"I want to, but there's just so much work inside to do still." He glanced at her. "It may have to wait until next year."

"You could always hire someone," she suggested.

His eyebrows shot up. "I suppose I could." He glanced around his yard again. "It's kind of a personal project, fixing this place up. I want to take my time. Put my own sweat and soul into it, you know?" He glanced at her and she smiled.

"Yeah, when I purchased my place, I did the same thing," she admitted. "It's the first place that has been mine." She leaned back and sipped her drink. "I wanted to put my mark on the home. To make it ours." She looked over at her daughter, who was watching one of her favorite TV shows on the iPad she had brought along. "I spent every free moment I had the first year we lived there repainting, planting, or, in the case of my bathroom, completely redoing everything." She smiled. "Now, it's home."

He glanced around and nodded slowly. "That's what I want for this place."

"Cookies," Simona interrupted them with a cheerful plea.

Todd laughed and stood up, then walked in the back door and came out with a box of cookies from the local bakery, Sweet Expectations. A brother and sister duo, Wyatt and Melissa Sharpe, had taken over the bakery recently, after their mother died of cancer.

"You bought cookies from Sweet Expectations?" she asked.

"I'm trying to support local." He shrugged. "Besides, I was in there yesterday on a much-needed donut run."

She smiled. "I wouldn't think that a man in your great shape ate too many sweets."

"Not too often. But since I've been burning through the calories working around the place, I've made an exception. Besides, they have really great sweets at the bakery."

She smiled. "Yes, they do."

"The town has grown so much from what I remember. About the only shop that is still the same is Serenity's Attic." He bit into a cookie.

She leaned back and munched on a cookie as she watched a few seagulls floating over the water. She couldn't get over the view. A cool breeze came off the water, and the smell of the salt in the air had her relaxing even more.

"The store is one of the longest running businesses in town. Crystal has been smart and has changed the store with the needs of the customers. Adding local produce and free-range eggs and meats was by far the best idea. We make almost as much on those products as we do on the touristy type items." She laughed. "A couple years back, Crystal was asked to do a couple star chart readings and now she takes requests. I swear if she could, she'd read palms."

He glanced at her. "Do you believe in that stuff?"

She shrugged. "No, not really." She tilted her head. "Although, she did predict that I'd meet you."

"Oh?" His eyebrows shot up.

She chuckled and waved her hand in the air.

"The morning we met." She looked over at him. "Crystal read my star chart and claimed that a child would find me love." She watched for his reaction and was slightly surprised when he didn't laugh the statement off.

CHAPTER 8

$\mathcal{T}$odd thought about Olivia's words. Thought about being free to find love. To have a normal life. Up until he'd received that text, he would have thought it was possible. Now, however, he was beginning to think that coming to Silver Cove was a mistake.

He wasn't free any longer. Not now that they knew where he was. Actually, he shouldn't be sitting out here in the wide open, with Olivia and her daughter, enjoying the evening air and grilling dinner like he had not a care in the world.

What he should be doing is packing up, changing his name and... he thought about hiding for the rest of his life and shook his head. That wasn't what he wanted. That was no way to live life.

He looked at Olivia and smiled. She easily matched his idea of the perfect woman. If he was free to live and love, that is.

"I'll have to start believing in star charts then," he said with a smile.

She remained quiet for a moment and then glanced over

to where Simona was fast asleep in the chair. The iPad continued to play the show she'd been watching.

"I'd better get her home," she said with a slight sigh.

He wanted to offer to bring Simona inside, to lay her on the sofa while they went into his room to… He took a deep breath and stood up.

"I'll help you carry her out to the car," he said while she gathered their things and piled it all into a massive bag.

He gently picked Simona up in his arms, careful not to wake her, and followed Olivia down the gravel pathway towards her car.

"Thank you," she said after he set her down in the car seat. "For today," she said after she secured Simona in the seat.

When she shut the car door, he pulled her into his arms and kissed her. This time he moved slowly, enjoying the taste of the chocolate and sugar on her lips. The feeling of her soft body against his. The way she melted in his arms.

He wanted to explore that feeling further but knew that Simona was sleeping just inside the car. When he pulled back, Olivia swayed slightly. He smiled when she leaned against the car, as if needing it to hold her upright.

"Thursday," he said, and her eyes cleared a little.

"Thursday." She nodded and turned to go.

"Can I get your number?" he asked before she left.

"Oh, I… um." She shook her head as if to clear it. "Yes, it's…" She started to rattle off a number, but then stopped and sighed. "I forgot. I just had it changed." She pulled out her cell phone and looked up her new number. She connected their phones and shared her contact with him.

"Thanks." He remembered what she'd said about her ex and sobered. "If you need anything. If you feel unsafe in any way, or if your ex…" He shook his head. "I'm a phone call away."

"Thank you." She touched his arm.

"Tell Simona I said goodnight." He glanced into the car.

"She'll be upset that she didn't get to say goodbye." Olivia smiled.

"Maybe I'll be lucky enough to run into the two of you again before Thursday," he suggested.

Olivia smiled. "You know where I work," she hinted. "And Simona and I like to play in the park on Wednesday afternoons when I get off work."

He nodded. "I like parks."

She laughed. "See you around." She got in her car, and he stood there, in the middle of the one-lane road, and watched her taillights disappear.

He had to admit, it was nice living on a point. One road in, only a handful of homes, no traffic. If anyone came around that didn't belong there, someone was bound to notice.

He glanced up and down the lane at the other homes around him. Most had lights on inside, a signal that his neighbors were inside enjoying their evenings. Still, it wouldn't hurt to have a new security system installed. Something state of the art.

He knew he had to call his CO and inform him about the text message. No doubt they'd want him to come in or sign up for some sort of protection.

He walked over to the back of his house and looked out over the sea wall towards the small town of Silver Cove. This was where he wanted to be. Where he'd hoped to build a home, to have a family, to spend the rest of his life. Now, after that text message, he was thinking of taking off again and that thought sank in his stomach like a stone.

He didn't want to leave. He didn't want to hide. He wanted to see Olivia and Simona at the park tomorrow. He wanted to take Olivia out on a date the following night and kiss her again. Maybe even a little more.

That thought had him smiling. Pulling out his phone, he shot a text message to his CO and informed him of the message he'd received. Before he could step inside his house, his cell phone was ringing.

Carl Harper, his commanding officer was one of the most straightforward men Todd had ever met. Straightforward and intense.

"Are you packing?" Carl asked when he answered the phone.

"No, I'm sticking." He locked the door and walked around to make sure the house was secure. "I'm going to invest in a security system in the morning."

"Don't bother. I'll send my guy," Carl replied, and Todd could hear him typing. "I know you don't need it, but he'll be sticking around for a while. I hope you have a place to put him up."

Todd instantly wanted to argue that he didn't need to be babysat, but then he thought about the three other people in his team that had thought the same thing. Three other members that he'd watched being lowered into graves.

He glanced around the house and then thought about the room above the garage. "Yeah, I've got a place."

"Good, his name is Ethan Knight. He'll be there first thing in the morning," Carl said. "Until then, sleep light."

"Yeah," he agreed, wondering if he'd get any sleep at all. There had been plenty of nights that he'd gone without sleep in the past. "Thanks," he said before hanging up.

Morning seemed to take forever to come. He spent half of the night researching and trying to figure out who in his team's past would have the resources to find his crew and the money and reach to hunt them down one by one.

When he'd been in the service, he'd been responsible for

Roderick Murphy, AJ Collins, and Jamie Anderson. Their lives had been his responsibility. Losing one would have been tragic, but all three... it had been the reason for his early retirement.

If he'd lost any of them in the line of duty, he could have at least been a little consoled that they'd died for a cause. But having them hunted down in the real world, as they called it, had been far worse.

When Rodrick and his wife had died in a car accident, it hadn't sent up any red flags. After all, accidents happen. Right?

But less than a month later, AJ was shot in what appeared at first to be a botched mugging. A second death in his team had caused the hairs on the back of his neck to stand. He'd mentioned it to his CO, Carl, who had listened to his concerns and thankfully done something about it. By the time of AJ's burial service, Carl had information that there was more to Rodrick's accident than they'd thought. He'd also somehow gotten a hold of some grainy video of AJ's shooting that clearly showed it wasn't a simple mugging. The same van that had caused Rodrick's accident in Dallas had been used to snatch AJ off the street in Houston.

An hour before AJ's body was found on the sidewalk, a figure in all black had rushed out of a dark van, tased AJ, and quickly loaded him up in the back. Less than an hour later, they'd returned his body to the very same spot, dumping him like trash on the sidewalk.

The first thing Todd had done was to alert the rest of his team.

Jamie Anderson, the only female member under his control, was one of the members still out on active duty. She had been working in Asia on assignment, but when their concerns were raised, she was brought back to the States.

Within a month after AJ's death, she'd been kidnapped from her apartment in San Diego.

By the time he'd gotten there, they had already found her body, which had been dumped in the bay. Video surfaced of the same dark van pulling out of her apartment garage the night of the kidnapping.

Carl had wanted to place the rest of his team under protection. Since Todd had officially retired two months earlier, he'd headed to Silver Cove, knowing that his team was safe, never expecting he was on the hit list as well.

Retirement wasn't hard. After all, in the past few years on the job, he'd been dreaming of settling down and returning to Silver Cove.

But having three of his team members killed had made him wish he was back on the job to hunt down the bastard taking them out.

When his doorbell rang shortly after seven the next morning, he pulled out his gun and was ready for a fight. Then a man called out.

"Todd O'Brien? I'm Ethan Knight. Carl Harper sent me. I'm sending my credentials to the cell number Carl provided."

Todd opened the text message. After glancing over the information, he received another text from Carl.

"And Carl just sent you confirmation," Ethan said from behind his front door.

When Todd opened the door, he realized that if the man standing on his front porch had wanted to break in and kill him, he would have been dead moments ago.

To say the man was massive would be an understatement. The man towered over Todd's own six-foot height and was easily double his weight, with solid muscles.

"Todd." Ethan nodded and held out his hand. "Ethan Knight."

Todd shook the man's hand and opened his front door for him to enter. The man glanced back at a white van parked in front of his garage. "My teammate Javan is going to start setting up the security system."

Todd glanced out to see a black man almost as impressively large as Ethan unloading equipment from the back of the van.

"Sure," he answered. "I was going to set you up in the apartment above the garage." He motioned to the space.

"Keys?" Ethan asked.

Todd reached over and took a set of keys from the key ring by the front door and handed them to Ethan.

"I'll be a minute." He disappeared back down the pathway. Todd watched Ethan hand Javan the key ring and then motion towards the garage and the house before walking back and coming in the front door.

"Carl has filled me in on your situation," Ethan said, his eyes meeting his own. "I want you to know that we will do everything in our power to keep you safe."

"Thanks." Somehow hearing those words from the man made it all so much more real.

"First, I'll need you to fill me in on your life around here." He glanced around and then turned back to him. "I'll need to know about your job, your friends, who you're dating, sleeping with, every aspect of your life. Nothing can be left out." His eyes narrowed. "No secrets. Got it?"

Spending the day exposing his entire life to a stranger left Todd raw. He stood by and watched the two men completely wire his home. He'd had a brief talk with Javan, who spoke with a thick Jamaican accent. The older man was funnier than Ethan and always seemed to be cracking a joke, usually at Ethan's expense.

Todd found out through Javan that Ethan was married and had two kids ages five and seven back in Washington

State. Javan traveled around too much to have a home base and was, as he described it, married to the job.

New wiring was installed to compensate for the new electronic needs, and he watched as Javan rewired his breaker box, a task that had been on Todd's to-do list. He was shown how the new system worked, where the hidden cameras were, how to trip the alarm from any room in the house, and where to go if an emergency arose.

As he got ready to head to the park for his visit with Simona and Olivia, he realized that his private life was no longer private.

The dark SUV that Ethan had swapped the white van out for tailed him into town.

When he parked at the edge of the square and walked to the park to meet Olivia, the SUV was within sight.

Seeing Simona playing on the playground with a group of kids her age had him smiling. She was laughing and running around, being chased by a little boy in an obvious game of tag.

He spotted Olivia sitting on a park bench and watching him walk towards her and felt his smile grow.

"Afternoon." He sat down next to her and took her hand in his.

"Hi." She smiled back at him. "I wasn't sure you were going to make it."

His smile slipped slightly. "I was having my new security system installed this morning, which required some electric work." He rolled his eyes and tried to come off as casual about the whole ordeal. It was far too soon to confide in Olivia about his personal problems. Especially when it might mean that he was in danger now.

"So..." She leaned back against his arm slightly as she ran her eyes over him. "I was thinking about our date."

He smiled. "Oh?" He pulled her closer and wished that

they were alone somewhere, anywhere other than in front of a bunch of kids playing a few feet away.

"Yes, I was wondering if I should dress up or dress more casual."

He chuckled. "Casual. Definitely."

She nodded. "Is it a surprise?" she asked, her eyebrows arching.

"Do you like surprises?"

She chuckled. "Good ones, yes."

"Then you'll just have to wait and find out tomorrow night," he supplied, causing her to laugh.

"I can do casual." She relaxed against his shoulder.

"Tell me about your day so far," he said as he wrapped an arm around her. He listened to her talk about her morning at work, about Simona's adventures at Kayla's day care, and what she had planned for dinner and the evening.

To most it would have sounded boring. To him, it sounded wonderful. He wanted to take part in all of it. He wanted to hear Simona chatter on about her day, what she'd drawn or what games she'd played. He wanted to hear about Olivia's workday and help her plan to keep her daughter entertained for the evening.

When Simona spotted him, she rushed over and hugged him and then took over the conversation for a few moments until her friends called her back out to swing on the swing set.

When the sun started to get low, Olivia called Simona over and they packed up to head home for dinner.

Since he needed some more groceries, he made a stop and purchased some food. Ethan followed him inside and purchased a full load of groceries for him and Javan.

When he unloaded his groceries from his car, he could see a light in the rooms above the garage and was surprised when Javan appeared on the pathway to his front door.

"Everything all right, boss?" Javan asked, his white teeth almost glowing in the moonlight.

"Yes," he answered, letting the man take one of the bags of groceries from his hands. "Here?"

"All quiet. Everything is in place." He nodded, understanding that the man had gone through and installed two wall gun safes, one behind a picture in the living room and another one in the closet of the main bedroom upstairs. Since they had discussed that it would be better for him not to be on the bottom floor, he'd spent time earlier that day moving his things up to the main bedroom on the top floor.

It hadn't taken long to get the bedroom set up; the hardest part was moving the new mattress from downstairs up the two flights of stairs. But thanks to Ethan and Javan, it hadn't taken as much effort on his part.

After putting away his groceries, Javan and Ethan disappeared while he made himself a grilled cheese sandwich and heated up some soup. He took his food into the television room along with a beer and watched the sports channel until he started dozing off on the sofa. Then he shut everything off, locked up, and headed up the stairs to bed. He felt more at ease and slept a lot better that night, knowing that Ethan and Javan were out there, watching out for him.

CHAPTER 9

Silver Cove wasn't that small of a town. But still, the next morning at work, she heard the rumors about the two men who had moved into the apartment above Todd's garage the day before.

When she had a moment to sit behind the counter, she pulled out her cell phone and sent him a text.

"I heard you had two renters move in?"

His reply came almost ten minutes later.

"Yeah, we'll talk more about that tonight. Looking forward to seeing you. I'll pick you up at the store around six?"

"Six is good," she replied. She couldn't help smiling for the rest of her shift.

She'd brought along clothing so she could change out of the yoga pants and the top she'd worn to her morning yoga class. Clocking out when Cora arrived early, she headed back and utilized the showers in the changing room and quickly dressed in a cotton dress, a light blue sweater, and her favorite pair of sandals. She figured her outfit was just the right amount of casual. After fixing her hair and makeup, she put her bag into the office and locked up.

When she stepped into the main part of the store, Todd was already there, chatting with Cora about star charts.

When she noticed the bundle of flowers in his hands, she melted.

"For me?" she asked. She held in a giggle as he wrapped his arms around her waist.

"Yes." He brushed his lips over hers. "Cora was just reading my charts."

"Cora is terrible at reading charts," she teased. "She actually told me last month that I'd be taking a very long unexpected tropical trip." Olivia narrowed her eyes at her friend. "I'm still waiting for my airplane tickets to arrive."

Cora laughed. "It'll happen. Sooner or later," she joked back. "You two kids have fun tonight."

Cora was a year younger than Olivia, so her comment made her laugh. "Okay, Mom." She tugged on Todd's hand as they walked out of the store together. "So," she said when they were outside in the heat, "where to?"

He locked his fingers with hers and started strolling down the sidewalk. "First, I want you to know that I pulled some very serious strings to get us in this place tonight." He stopped suddenly and then pulled her into his arms. "So, I hope you don't mind if it's going to take a while before we eat."

She wrapped her arms around his shoulders and shook her head. "I had a late lunch," she told him, but her stomach silently growled, and she wished for an early dinner. Just to be with him, she'd fend off the starvation. For a while.

"Good." He leaned in and gently placed his lips over hers. "Second, I hate to do this to you, and I'll explain on the way, but we won't be traveling alone." He motioned to a rather large man leaning against a dark sedan.

She glanced over and narrowed her eyes as she assessed the man. He appeared a few years older than they were, a few inches taller than Todd, but easily double his build. The man's arms were as thick as Todd's thighs and full of muscles. Instantly, she felt intimidated.

"Bodyguard?" she asked with a frown.

Todd sighed and nodded slowly. "Of sorts. As I said, I'll explain on our way." He glanced down at his watch and started walking again. "Ethan will tag along with us, but don't worry, he won't be sitting at our table dining with us."

She followed him, quietly thinking, as they made their way towards the docks. Ethan followed them down the docks.

Seeing the ferry in its normal spot, she smiled.

"Are we heading to East Haven for dinner?" Excitement flooded her voice.

Todd smiled. "It's the best place around. Besides, I hear Adam's food is worth the trip and the price. I hope it's okay?"

"Yes." She nodded. "I've been dying for his quenelles of pike with lobster sauce. It's one of my favorites." She let him help her onto the ferry.

"Evening, Todd," she said to the man who ran the ferry. Then she turned to Todd and smiled. "Todd, Todd." She motioned between the two men.

Todd laughed. "When I met Simona, she was upset that I was lying about my name," he said, shaking the other Todd's hand.

"As she put it, I wasn't Todd, because she knew Todd." He chuckled.

The other Todd chuckled. "Simona's one of a kind. How is she?" he asked, standing back to let Ethan on the ferry.

"She's great. We're going to have to head out to the resort soon and take a day to go swimming so you can see her again," Olivia said to the other man.

"Ethan's with us," Todd said easily. "Ethan Knight, Olivia Scott, and this is the other Todd in Silver Cove."

"There's actually four of us," Todd said as he locked the gate behind them and then headed up the stairs that led to the captain's cabin of the ferry. "Todd Rogers is about a hundred years old and spends half his time playing checkers in the library or park. And Todd Fletcher." Todd glanced back as he paused halfway up the stairs. "He's eight and thinks that girls have cooties." He winked at Olivia and then turned to finish heading up the stairs.

She shook her head. "Todd is by far the biggest flirt in town."

"Yet you never fell for his tricks?" Todd asked, leaning against the railing as the ferry slowly backed out of the dock.

"No." She smiled. "He's good-looking enough, but I like my men…" She ran her eyes over him slowly and then tilted her head slightly. "A little more mysterious and dangerous."

Something shifted in his eyes, and he took a deep breath as his hand ran over her arm slowly.

She'd noticed that Ethan had headed up the stairs behind Todd, leaving them alone on the main deck of the ferry. She knew that the slow ferry ride to the private island that held the swanky East Haven Resort would take roughly twenty minutes. Plenty of time to get the story from Todd.

"You know that I was Special Ops and that I retired a couple months back," he started.

She nodded. "Yes, you told me as much." She tried to encourage him to continue.

"Shortly before I retired, a few of my team…" He closed his eyes briefly, before turning fully towards her. "They were killed."

She frowned. "I'm so sorry."

He shook his head. "Not in the line of duty. They were killed while in the real world. Off duty. Civilians."

"Okay," she said slowly.

"Someone is targeting my team. Ethan and his partner Javan are here just as a precaution," Todd explained.

She wanted to ask more but could see that he was trying desperately not to let this spoil their date.

"Are you safe?" she asked, worried for him.

"We've taken all the precautions." He smiled. "I have a new security system, two very skilled ex-military men watching out for my six and"—he leaned a little closer and lowered his voice as he ran a hand over her shoulder— "I want to remind you that I didn't make sergeant because of my winning smile."

She laughed as he showed her that sexy smile of his. "I don't know; that smile is something." She moved closer and wrapped her arms around his shoulders.

When he kissed her, she felt her entire body become lighter than air. Maybe it was the fact that it was the first time she'd been kissed while on a boat, or maybe it was because it was Todd. Either way, she enjoyed the floating sensation for as long as she could, holding onto him as he slowly unraveled all the worry and stress from her day.

When the ferry pulled into the smaller dock at East Haven, there was a golf cart waiting to take them up to the massive white building. She couldn't count the number of times she and Simona had been to the resort over the past few years. More so since her divorce.

In the summers, they'd head out here with the other families and spend time at the pool or beach. In the winter months, there were holiday balls or plays and family events such as hayrides or sleigh rides in the snow. But she'd never been out here for a romantic date. After they'd gotten married, Brock had never believed in going out on dates. Not with her, at any rate.

Tonight, there were firefly lights hanging from all of the

low tree branches, lighting the way up the pathway towards the building.

She was slightly surprised when the golf cart didn't stop at the wide porch and instead continued to head down the pathway towards the larger pool. Here, more string lights hung over small tables that had crisp white tablecloths. They had been placed all around the pool deck area. There were other couples dining by candlelight while waiters and waitresses moved silently around, seeing to every need of their guests.

They were shown to a table closest to the water, overlooking the dark waters beyond the grassy yard. With the sun setting, the entire sky was lit up in pastel pinks and purples.

"Wow, I didn't know they had set tables out here for dinner," Olivia said as he pulled out her chair for her.

"I ran into Sarah at the store yesterday, and she suggested that we give it a try since it's their first week serving dinners outside." He sat down across from her.

"I like it. I think it's a marvelous idea." She took a deep breath of the fresh salty air and glanced around.

"Mix great atmosphere with amazing food and they'll have a winning duo," he agreed. "Wine?"

She leaned slightly on the table. "I like dry," she said, looking at a little chalk board on their table, showing the selections.

"Ditto." He chuckled. "You pick."

She normally didn't compare men to Brock, but just having a man who enjoyed the same wine as she did and enjoyed talking about the same topics was a relief. She couldn't remember ever talking to Brock about her work, her dreams, or even Simona's future. They ordered food and continued talking. Even when it was delivered, the conversation flowed.

She voiced her concerns as a mother about her daughter getting the best education, the best jobs, and even finding the perfect mate.

Todd asked about Simona's hobbies, if she was interested in anything special, and Olivia had to admit that she didn't know herself.

"She likes to color, to watch her shows." She frowned down into her meal.

"She liked pretending to be a teacher in my old classroom."

She smiled and nodded. "She did."

"You know, I never really got to express my interests as a child. When my father was alive, he was molding me to take over his business. After his death, my mother showed zero interest in my life. I often wish I'd had someone to encourage me."

"What did you want to be?" she asked, curious. Her own parents hadn't shown much interest in her future, either. There had been times when she'd been very young that she wanted to dance, then ride horses, and when she'd hit high school, she'd thought about becoming a nurse or a doctor. But then she'd voiced those dreams and her parents had informed her that they wouldn't be paying for anything but community college. Where she'd met Brock.

"When I was younger? I wanted to be a businessman like my father." Todd took a sip of his wine. "After his death, my mother sold his business."

"Which was?" she asked.

"He owned several large rental properties, grocery stores chains, and—my favorite—he owned a football team. My dad wasn't really the outdoor type, but he did love sports."

"Brock used to think I was weird for watching football." She remembered him teasing her that girls shouldn't enjoy sports as much as men. "I've always enjoyed watching men run around in tights after a ball," she joked, and he smiled.

"Did you play sports?" he asked.

"Soccer when I was younger, but after my parents found out that they'd have to shuttle me around the first year, they made me quit."

"They're still in Chicago?"

"Yeah." She took a sip of her wine after finishing off her dinner.

"What do they do?"

"My father is a manager at a bank, and my mother is a teacher at the local high school. I often thought it was ironic that she enjoyed teaching other people's kids more than her own daughter." She tried to hide the disdain in her voice. Apparently, she failed.

"Sounds like you don't get along with them?"

"They haven't met Simona," she threw out, and then wondered why, since she'd tried to convince herself that it wasn't a big deal. After all, Simona had Crystal and Rory to fill in as grandparents. At least that's what she tried to convince herself of.

"They haven't?" Todd grew quiet and then leaned back in his chair. "What do you say to a stroll around the place?"

She smiled. "I'd love to."

The private island that the resort sat on was large enough to house a small golf course, three swimming pools, a private sandy beach, large garden areas equipped with many ponds, and gazebos for special events. Besides the four-story white Colonial building, which housed over two hundred rooms, it had separate buildings for employee housing and a smaller building used for a spa and pool house.

The place sat on one of the largest islands off the coast of Maine. Olivia had walked every square inch of the island and loved it all. Her favorite by far was the soft sandy beach. She and Simona often came out here on their free days and soaked up the sun or had picnics in the sand.

She and Todd made their way out of the main pool area, closest to the house, and walked down the path that led to one of the smaller pools.

"Have any idea where this path leads?" he asked her, taking her hand in his.

"The smaller pool."

"They have more than one pool?" he asked. "I guess I only remember the one." He motioned behind them.

She chuckled. "Three in total. One is more for younger kids or a wading pool. This one has the hot tub."

His eyebrows shot up. "I don't suppose you brought a swimsuit?"

She laughed. "No, did you?"

He shook his head. "No, but a soak in a hot tub sounds amazing, with all the work I've been doing around the house." He shrugged. "I suppose I could look at getting one for my place."

They stopped at the jacuzzi and watched the steam floating up from the hot water, and she had to admit, the hot tub bubbles would probably feel amazing. Then, without questioning herself any further, she toed off her sandals and smiled at him.

"I didn't bring a suit, but women's undergarments are basically swimwear." She shrugged and ran her eyes over him, dreaming of what he was wearing underneath his button-up shirt and khaki pants.

He smiled and slowly started unbuttoning his shirt while she removed the cardigan and her dress.

Their eyes were glued to one another as they slowly stripped off their clothes and set them on a chair next to the hot tub.

In the dim light of the pool, she enjoyed the sight of his

lean toned body. My god, most of the man was muscle. She doubted he had an ounce of fat on him. She started to second-guess her decision, since her body was... well, lacking next to his. She'd had a kid after all. It wasn't as if she was flabby, but parts of her weren't where or as they used to be.

Then his eyes ran over her body, taking in her cream-colored matching bra and panties, and she watched heat and desire flood his gaze, causing her to relax. Brock had claimed that, after Simona, her body no longer turned him on. But over the past few years, she'd dropped the extra weight she'd gained during her pregnancy and had toned up a lot, thanks to the yoga and days she spent at the gym.

Todd stepped into the hot tub and then held a hand for hers. The hot water caused her to hiss and then moan as she sank down below the bubbles.

"My god," Todd said beside her as he leaned his head back against the side. "This was by far the best idea." He glanced over at her with a smile. "Best second date ever." He took her hand under the water and squeezed lightly, then tugged her closer and wrapped an arm around her shoulders. "Now this is nice." He sighed and relaxed back.

She leaned her head against his shoulder and wondered if she'd ever felt this comfortable around any other man this quickly before. Todd was by far the easiest person to talk to. He somehow understood her sense of humor when she'd joked with him over dinner and wasn't afraid to be around her or Simona.

The fact that he was up front with her about what he was going through made her want to open up a little more to him about her past. About what Brock had put her through all the years they'd been together.

Then his hand started moving up her arm and her mind shifted gears as desire had her body shaking.

"Todd?" she said, turning her body towards him, letting her hands run slowly up his chest.

"Hm," he asked, his eyes locked with her lips.

"Do you think…" She smiled when his hands cupped her hips and hoisted her up onto his lap. Just the hardness of the man underneath her had her inner muscles aching and turning her legs to jelly. "Do you think that we'll have enough time alone to…" She leaned in and brushed her lips across his and felt his response under the water. She wanted nothing more than to slide onto the hardness she felt under his boxer briefs. To ride him until she felt the sweet release that she'd been missing for so long.

"Olivia," he groaned, not removing his lips from hers. "I want you so much, but I think…" He glanced around and lowered his voice. "I know that Ethan is out there, somewhere, watching over us."

She stiffened. She'd totally forgotten about his bodyguard and almost dunked her head under the water in response. Todd chuckled and held her still.

"Easy. I've been told by his partner that the man is, as he put it, stupidly in love with his wife," Todd added, making Olivia smile.

What would it feel like to be that far in love with someone that even your friends knew it? Would she ever feel that much for a man? Could she ever trust someone that much after what she'd been through? Then she felt Todd's hands move over her skin and she decided she was already starting to fall for a man she'd only known for a few days. How was that even possible?

CHAPTER 10

Todd would have easily taken Olivia right then and there. Hell, in the past, he wouldn't have thought twice. But with her, here, now, he wanted things to be different. She mattered more than anyone else had in his past.

Yet, he didn't want to sound like a fool by telling her this. Instead, he had made some excuse about Ethan being out there, which was true. Still, that knowledge wouldn't have stopped him in the past.

That didn't mean, however, that they couldn't still enjoy themselves. The hot tub was doing wonders to relax a few aches he'd gotten over the past few weeks working on the house.

With Olivia rubbing against him, his mind was focused on how wonderful her tight little body felt. His hands roamed slowly up and down her body and when he cupped her breasts, she released the sexiest moan he'd ever heard.

"Do you like that?" he asked softly.

"My god, it's been so… long," she said, her eyes closed. She rolled her head back as he pinched her nipples between his fingers. She arched into him and he nudged the wet see-through material aside to dip his head down and run his mouth over her soft skin.

She buried her fingers in his hair, holding him closer as he lapped at her skin. The mixture of her perfume and the salt water was intoxicating. His hands roamed lower to grip her hips as she started grinding against him. His dick jumped as it pushed against her softness.

He couldn't remember ever wanting someone this badly before. His finger covered her, rubbed against her, and then dipped just under the soft silk of her panties to find her warm, waiting for him. She sucked in her bottom lip and held it between her teeth as he enjoyed the feeling of her tightening around his fingers.

Just imagining what she would feel like wrapped around him almost made him come. How could a woman do this to him?

Her hips moved slowly as she rode his fingers, and just watching her as she took her pleasure from him had him groaning. Then he watched in amazement as she arched back, bit her bottom lip and came for him.

"My god," he said, pulling her lips back down to his in a kiss that seared him down to his soul. "You're amazing."

She leaned against his chest, those perfect breasts of hers pushed up against his chest as her breathing and heartbeat settled. He could almost hear her thinking when she stiffened and realized what he'd done to her and where they were.

He chuckled. "I take it you've never done anything like that in a public setting before?" he asked.

She shook her head. "My god, I don't think I'll ever be able to look at Ethan again."

His laughed again and wrapped his arms around her. "I want to do this again with you soon. Someplace we can be alone." He nudged her until she sat up and met his eyes. "All night."

She nodded. "I'd like that."

"For now, what do you say we sit back and let these bubbles relax us, before we head back to town."

She shifted to sit beside him. She ran her hand over his chest, making small little circles around his flat nipples while her other hand found him, still hard under the water. "Don't you think it's only fair that I return the favor?" she asked, gripping him firmly. His eyes crossed and then closed as she started stroking him.

He opened his mouth to tell her that she didn't have to, but then he swallowed the words when she nudged his shorts down and started stroking him, skin to skin.

She moved until her lips brushed against his ear. "Do you like this?" she asked.

His fingers tightened in her hair as he pulled her back to his lips to kiss her while she continued to please him.

"You're a witch," he said later as they dressed again by the pool.

She chuckled. "Maybe I am." She looked over her shoulder at him. "If I was, I'd cast a spell and make us the only two people on the island so we could have all night together."

He'd pulled on his pants and held his shirt in his hands. Before putting it on, he walked over and wrapped his arms around her and kissed her one more time.

"Whatever spells you have, I'd gladly let you cast them on me." He kissed her again.

Just then, they both heard the laughter of people making their way towards the pool area.

Olivia nudged him aside and quickly pulled on her dress and sweater.

She was just putting on her sandals and he was tying his shoes when three couples came walking onto the pool deck.

"Evening," he said casually.

The couples looked at them and smiled. "Oh, evening," one of the women said with a giggle. "I hope we didn't interrupt anything?"

"No." He smiled and helped Olivia stand, making a point to hold onto her hand. "We were just enjoying the bubbles." He nodded to the hot tub. "Have a good night." He nodded to the couples and started slowly walking back down the pathway towards the docks.

"What do you say we stop off at the kitchen? I could use some dessert," Olivia said.

"The kitchen?"

She laughed. "Tara, the pastry chef, is a friend. She bakes for the bakery in town and works out here as well. She always has extra cookies or pie on hand."

"I could go for some pie," he agreed, changing their direction.

They sat out on the massive front deck of the resort while he enjoyed a piece of chocolate silk pie and she ate a bowl of chocolate brownie delight, which consisted of chocolate brownie, caramel topping, chopped walnuts, whipped cream, and some more caramel chunks on top.

He gave her a bite of his pie and, after getting a bite of her brownie, had to admit she'd picked the best dessert.

It was all so casual, the way they fell into conversation easily, changing between topics ranging from work, sports, Simona, or their pasts. He didn't feel the need to hide anything from her, which was in itself rewarding since he'd spent years lying to everyone.

The ferry ride back to town went by too quicky, and the entire ride back he dreamed of the evening not ending. But he knew that with Ethan tagging along, he'd have to cut the night short.

He walked her to her car and kissed her under a streetlight while Ethan sat in the dark SUV. When he climbed into the seat next Ethan, the man turned to him.

"You know, you can act like we're not here," the man said casually.

Todd laughed. "Right." He sighed. "I have no problem with it, but something tells me Olivia was having a hard time with it."

They drove through the sleepy town, heading towards his place.

"Maybe next time she has a night off, just invite her over to your place? It's probably best for security purposes anyway," he suggested.

It wasn't a bad idea. But he hadn't wanted her to feel like he was moving too fast.

When he was lying in his new bedroom, staring up at the ceiling, he pulled out his phone and sent her a text message.

"I had a great time tonight."

Her response came instantly.

"Me too. Thank you. Dinner, adult conversation, and the bubbles were just what I needed."

"I needed you. It's been a while since I've been able to open myself up like this. I promise next time we go out, you won't even notice Ethan."

"Maybe next time, I'll just come over to your place and we can have a night in?"

He felt his heart skip as he typed his response.

"I'd like that. When's your next free night?"

It took her a moment to answer this one.

"I can arrange for Simona to spend the night at Crystal and Rory's next Thursday."

"It's a date. I'll cook, you bring the dessert."

She sent an emoji of red lips and champagne glasses.

"Night," he replied.

"Goodnight."

The weekend went by in a blur. He worked on clearing out the rest of the rooms in the house, which included hauling out a few pieces of furniture that were old or outdated and ordering a couple small items from a local store.

He ran into Rowan a few more times at the hardware store, and the two of them seemed to hit it off pretty well. Rowan invited him over for Sunday brunch and the game. He almost declined due to Ethan or Javan having to tag along but decided that his life couldn't stop because there was a possibility of someone out to get him. Besides, after the first text message, he hadn't gotten any more.

Then again, no strange messages had been sent to any of his other team members prior to their murders. His CO was sure the message was a fluke, since they had tracked the burner cell it had come from somewhere in Georgia.

When Sunday rolled around, he had not only finished clearing and cleaning out all the rooms upstairs, but he'd ordered the new carpet that was to be installed in less than a week and had started replacing the old wood flooring on the stairs.

It was a process, but when he was done, instead of run-down carpet on the two sets of stairs, there would be dark maple hardwood and new maple railings leading all the way up to the top floor. He planned to sand and restain the hardwood on the main floor to match it.

He really liked the rustic look of the place and wanted to carry that atmosphere throughout the entire house, not just the main floor.

He stopped in town to grab a case of beer and headed to the address Rowan had given him.

Rowan's house was big and had a classic appearance, just like the two-story homes surrounding it. It was painted a soft beige with crisp white trim and had bright blue shutters. The yard was well maintained with bright flowers on each step leading up to the double stained-glass doors.

If Todd had to describe the house in one word, it would have been cheerful.

The last thing he expected after ringing the doorbell was to have Olivia answer the door, holding a bald-headed baby decked out in the smallest Maine Sea Dog's uniform he'd ever seen.

"Hi," she said with a smile. "Rowan told me he'd invited you." She swung the door open wide. "We're all in the back." She nodded for him to enter.

"Who is this?" he asked, brushing a finger down the little boy's chubby cheek.

"This is Emylia," she answered as she bounced the baby on her hip.

Little girl, he mentally corrected.

"Her daddy gets to dress her on game days." Olivia rolled her eyes and then leaned closer. "I think Adam secretly wished for another son."

He chuckled. "Girls can play sports too."

"Oh, I know it." She chuckled. "I'm way better at softball than Adam, but don't tell him I told you." She shut the front door as he stepped inside. "Fragile male ego and all." She shifted the kid on her hip and started walking back through the house. They passed through a very tidy living room and kitchen and then stepped out into what he could only describe as the most perfect backyard patio he'd ever seen.

There was a large-screen television hanging behind a large bar area that easily sat ten people. A circular patio table sat in the shade from umbrellas and the massive trees that shadowed the entire area.

A tall firepit table sat directly in the middle of the patio next to a large L-shaped sofa where several women with kids sat talking. Kids ran around the neatly trimmed grassy areas and played on a wooden swing set. A couple of boys played soccer, and most of the men were gathered around the bar area, either grilling or sipping beers and watching the game.

"Wow," he said softly.

Olivia chuckled. "Yeah, they fixed the backyard up a few years ago. I can only dream of having a yard as awesome as this one day." She walked over to hand the baby to Lilly, Adam's wife.

"Want a beer?" she asked.

He held up the case. "I brought some, but if there's some that are cold…"

She waved him over, and he followed her to the bar area.

"Todd's here," she called out.

"Todd!" several of the men cheered, causing him to laugh.

"Sorry." Olivia rolled her eyes. "They think they're in an episode of *Cheers*." She motioned him behind the bar and showed him where a large double-wide beer fridge was. He grabbed a cold beer of his liking and stacked his beer in an empty spot on the fridge so it would get cold.

"Burgers are on. They'll be ready in about fifteen," Rowan called over to him. "Make yourself at home."

Todd glanced around and noticed Simona playing with CJ now.

"Looks like they mended things," he said, sipping his beer as she took up a glass of wine and sipped.

"Yeah, their fights never last long." She sighed.

"That's good." He shifted a little closer. "This is a nice surprise, having you two here today."

Olivia smiled. "It's the first day of the season. It's a standing invitation. Rowan mentioned that he'd run into you at the hardware store and invited you when I got here. I would have, but…" She shrugged. "It wasn't my place."

"I'm just glad I needed a new O ring for the upstairs toilet," he joked.

"Oh? Having issues with the bathrooms upstairs?"

"No, just a leaky toilet, which I fixed on my own." He sighed. "After watching more than a dozen YouTube videos. The plumbers and electricians I hired are due to start work soon."

She laughed. "You'll get the hang of it." She touched his arm and then glanced around. "No Ethan?"

"He's around." He nodded. "After running a complete background check on Rowan and, well, anyone else he's related to, he determined it was safe enough for me to come today. Honestly, I think the text massage was just a fluke. After talking to my commanding officer, we both agree that the threat I received didn't fit the MO."

"Oh?" She motioned to a bench and they walked over to sit down under the shade of a large apple tree that held hundreds of small green apples not quite ready yet.

"Yeah, the message I received could have been from anyone. They found the burner phone it had been sent from in Georgia." He felt her stiffen next to him but continued on. "The message was vague enough that it could have been sent to me by mistake."

"What did it say?" she asked, her voice so low that he almost didn't hear her.

He pulled out his phone and showed her the message.

"Found you."

She closed her eyes and he watched in horror as all of the color left her cheeks.

"Hey, what's all this?" he asked, gathering her in his arms.

"It's from Brock," she said into his shoulder. "That message is from my ex-husband."

CHAPTER 11

Olivia felt all of her energy drain from her body. Her head felt light, and she was having a difficult time breathing. Had it been this hot outside earlier?

"Hey." Todd's voice sounded distant. "Focus on me," he said in a soothing voice. Something cold was shoved into her hand, and Todd helped her sip the water.

She heard other voices, but it wasn't until she heard Crystal's soothing voice that she shook herself out of it and was able to speak. "There now, what's going on here?"

"I'm… not sure," Todd said.

Wiping the tears from her eyes, she looked around and realized she was surrounded by concerned friends. Her makeshift family.

"I…" She swallowed and shook her head, then met Todd's eyes. "Brock likes to play games."

"Okay," he said, a frown causing his eyebrows to furrow.

She swallowed. "Especially hide and seek. Found you. It's his sick way of telling me that he's found out something about me." She motioned to her phone. She pulled up the screenshot of the text message that she'd received from Brock and handed it to Todd.

Todd read the words and sighed.

"You think Brock is the one who texted me?" he asked.

"It's the same. He sent this to me from a burner phone in Georgia."

"How do you…" He shook his head.

"I found that bit of information out." Rory stepped forward. "I know a guy who… well, at any rate, I know a guy."

Todd turned back to Olivia, and she could tell he was assessing her.

"Hey." He gathered her into his arms and held on. It felt so good to be held by a man who cared. A man she knew would never play games with her. "It's okay. I'll have Ethan look into—"

"Let her go." A strong little voice had them both looking over.

Simona stood, her little hands fisted by her side, her eyes glaring at him. If Olivia didn't know better, she would have sworn her daughter was on the verge of attacking Todd.

"Let my mommy go. Don't you hurt her," Simona added, her voice shaky this time.

She wanted to scold her daughter but knew that she was only trying to protect her.

"Simona," Olivia said in a calm voice. "Todd was just helping me. I wasn't feeling well."

Still, Todd dropped his arms from around her and scooted back on the bench, away from her a little.

"He made you cry," Simona said, moving closer, her eyes still on Todd.

"No, honey." Olivia grabbed up her daughter and put her on her lap. "He was comforting me because I was crying." She felt Simona relax in her arms. "I think you owe Todd an apology."

"No." Todd shook his head. "She was just standing up for her mother." He took Simona's hand. "Don't ever apologize for sticking up for someone you love. Okay?"

Simona glanced at her, and she smiled and wiped the rest of her tears off her face before nodding her head in agreement.

"Okay," Simona said, turning back to Todd. "I thought… I didn't like it when he hit her."

She noticed then that everyone had given them space, so it was only the three of them in the little garden area.

"Who?" Todd asked. "Your dad?"

Simona nodded as she looked up at her mother. Olivia had a hand over her mouth and the tears were back. She'd always believed she'd hidden Brock's abuse from her daughter. How had she allowed herself to be so naive? Of course Simona had known. How could she not?

"He broke her arm and she had to go to the hospital." Simona took her hand and lifted it, then ran her little fingers over the tiny white scars left by the pins she'd had to have. "She had… pins?" It was more a question than a statement, and Olivia nodded slightly. "They came out here," Simona continued, "and I couldn't touch her there or hold her hand because she was hurt. I won't let anyone hurt her again. She's my mommy." Her heart melted and hurt at the same time. Love for her daughter flooded her to the point that more tears started rolling down her cheeks.

"Not every man is like your dad," Todd began. "I would never hurt you or your mother." He held out his hand and Simona looked at it for a moment. "I promise you. I don't hit girls. Only bad guys hurt girls."

Simona's eyes moved up to his. "Promise?" He nodded

and Simona smiled as she put her tiny hand in his. "Okay." She turned back to her as she shook his hand and asked, "Why were you crying then?"

"Oh, honey." Olivia wrapped her arms around her daughter again. "I was being silly."

"Like when you cry during the car commercial?" Simona asked.

Olivia chuckled. "Yes, just like that." Olivia's eyes met Todd's over her daughter's head. "Hey, don't judge me. It's a powerful commercial."

He smiled. "Feeling better?" he asked.

Olivia's eyes shifted away from his, but she nodded. "Simona, why don't you go see if Kayla can get you a hot dog and some chips?"

"Okay." Simona climbed off her lap, and then turned and reached out to hug Todd. "I'm sorry I thought you hurt my mommy."

Todd's eyes closed as he held onto her little girl for a moment before letting her go. They both watched as she skipped across the yard towards Kayla and the rest of the kids, who were currently eating.

She turned and watched him closely as he smiled seeing Simona interact with the other kids.

"Do you really think it could be your ex?" he asked, turning back to her.

She thought about it, about all the times Brock had sent those same words to her, over and over, every time he'd believed he'd caught her in a lie or cheating. She nodded her head slowly.

"Why? I mean, we weren't, hadn't..." He shook his head. "We'd only run into each other a few times by then."

"That doesn't matter. Brock used to be jealous of any man I talked to." She glanced around. "It confirms my suspicion that he's either close by or has a buddy watching me." She leaned back in the bench and crossed her arms over her chest. "Eric and Brock have been best friends since grade school." She glanced out over the flowers surrounding them. "Eric works in town at the gas station."

She thought about the only man in town that had not believed her side of the story when Brock had broken her arm. For the first couple months after Brock had been arrested, Eric harassed her so much that she'd stopped using that gas station and had made a point to drive out of town to get her gas. She still did to this day.

Then she thought about what this could mean for Todd. If it was Brock who had sent that text instead of a madman out to kill him and his team.

"If it was Brock instead of…"—she lowered her voice—"the person who killed the members of your team, what does that mean?" Did it mean that his security team would leave? Somehow, she'd felt safer with them in town. If someone, someday could come after Todd, she wanted to know that he was safe.

"That means that I need to give my CO a call." They both glanced over when everyone cheered on the game on the set. "Go on over, grab some food. I'll make a quick call and be over."

She understood that he wanted to be alone for the call and stood up and walked over to her friends. She was instantly engulfed in a few hugs, then she sat next to her daughter with a plate full of food.

From across the yard, she watched him pull out his phone and talk as he paced the small grassy area.

When he was done, he joined the rest of them at the bar and tables and ate while cheering the game on.

When the sun started to set, Simona was sitting in Todd's

lap on the sofa while she sat next to them surrounded by her friends. When she noticed her daughter's head rolling as she started falling asleep, she suggested that it was time they head home.

Todd stood up, easily shifting Simona into his arms, and carried her daughter to her car. She watched as Todd gently placing Simona in her car seat and then stood back so Olivia could strap her daughter in and shut the door. She turned towards him, and he pulled her into his arms and gently kissed her.

"I'm glad you came today," she said with a slight sigh.

"Me too." He smiled. "Besides our team losing, today was a very lucky day. I'd like tomorrow to be even luckier."

She smiled and wrapped her arms around his shoulders. "Mondays are my days off. Simona and I were going to head out to find a spot for a picnic. You're welcome to tag along."

"Sounds perfect." He sighed when his cell phone rang in his pocket.

"I'll text you the details," she said and moved to get into her car. He stopped her by giving her one more kiss that had her toes curling.

"Night," he said before answering the call.

The entire short drive home, she played over the highlights of the day, how wonderful it had been to have a man enjoy her friends. Brock had shied away from hanging out with anyone she knew. Most of the time, she'd been stuck listening to him and his friends, usually Eric, play video games or drink themselves silly. They'd never hung out with other married couples. It was nice, being around other people that she had things in common with.

Getting Simona shuffled into the house used up the rest of her energy. When her daughter was safely tucked in her bed fast asleep, Olivia decided a nice long bath and one more glass of wine was just what she needed.

She always had a jar of Crystal's bath salts or some of her bath bombs on hand and dropped some into the water. The water turned a soft purple color as the scent of lavender filled the room. She poured herself a glass of wine and slid under the warm water and wished more than anything that she was back on the island with Todd, sitting in the hot tub.

Smiling, she pulled out her phone and sent him a text message of her toes poking out of the water next to the candle she'd lit.

"Wishing it was bubbles from a hot tub with you beside me."

She set the phone down after a few moments when he didn't reply, figuring he must be fast asleep. She'd just relaxed back when his reply came.

A picture almost matching hers flashed on her screen. His feet poked out of clear water, and instead of a candle, it was a flashlight.

"Sorry, I couldn't find any candles. But yeah, wishing I could be there too."

She laughed and then sank a little under the water.

"I'd ask you what you're wearing, but I can imagine instead," his next text said.

"You could always stop by the store Tuesday for early morning yoga and get some candles," she texted back.

"You won't get too tired of seeing me? That'll be three days in a row."

"I think I can handle it." She smiled as she replied.

"Then it's a date. Still not sure about the yoga, but if it means I get to see you in one of those sexy tight outfits, then I'm game."

She laughed and started typing. "Are you really taking a bath?"

"Yeah, I find it helps with sore muscles. A little Epsom salt and I'm good to go."

"We sell some bath salts you can add to the water that will help as well."

"Always the salesperson. You'll have to show me what I'm missing. Is Simona asleep?" he asked.

"Yeah, out like a light. Playing with her friends usually knocks her out quickly."

"I have to admit, I'm pretty tired myself. I had fun today. I'm sorry if you were upset."

"Did you hear anything back on that?" she asked.

"Not yet. I'll let you know the moment I do. Ethan seems to think it makes sense, though."

She closed her eyes and imagined the last time they were alone.

"I wish we had more time alone," she typed. She deleted it then typed it again and hit send.

"Me too. We're alone now. I wish I could run my hands over your wet body. I bet you smell amazing, sexy, and you're all soft and relaxed."

"I wish that too. I rather enjoy seeing you without a shirt on," she admitted.

"Those sexy bra and panties you wore in the hot tub are forever branded in my mind. Did you know that, when they were wet, they were see-through?"

She smiled. "I knew."

"My god," he replied. Then he sent another message, "I'm imagining running my hands over you."

She slowly ran her free hand over her body and closed her eyes, imagining it was Todd.

She jumped slightly when her phone rang. Seeing his number, she smiled and answered the call.

"There, now I can at least hear you," he said, and she heard water splashing around him.

She put her phone up to her ear and smiled as he talked to

her, telling her everything he'd like to do to her as she followed along with her own hands.

She couldn't stop herself from moaning his name when she felt her release flood through her. She smiled when she heard his release and her name on his lips.

"I wish I could kiss you good night," he said.

"Me too."

"Sleep tight. Dream of me."

"I will. We'll see you tomorrow." She smiled.

"I'll pick the both of you up around eleven," he said before hanging up.

When she crawled into bed, she was so relaxed and tired that she didn't hear her phone chime with a new message.

Her morning started out with her daughter standing over her bed, puking.

"Mommy, I don't feel good," Simona had said right before projectile vomiting all over her sheets and comforter.

She rushed her daughter into the bathroom just in time for a second round and held onto her while she leaned over the toilet this time. Rubbing Simona's back slowly, she felt her own insides curl at the sounds and smell. Still, she forced herself to hold on, to bear with it for her daughter's sake.

When Simona was done, she pulled off her soiled clothes and ran a bath for her.

"You lay in here," she said, after washing her daughter's hair and body. "I'm going to go clean up and get the laundry started."

"I'm sorry I puked all over your bed," Simona said softly.

"Sweetie, it's okay, it happens. You rest here, I'll be back." She made sure the water was shallow enough that Simona could lay her head down and not drown.

Leaving her in the bathroom, she rushed around and pulled both her and Simona's sheets and blankets off the bed and started the washing machine before she pulled out her phone and shot Todd a text message.

"Simona woke up sick this morning. I hate to do it, but we need to cancel today's picnic."

She went to set her phone down, but then noticed the other text message.

"I won't be ignored, slut. Do you think you can hide who you're fucking from me? I know everything that's going on. I'll get you for ruining my life."

With shaky hands she replied. "Brock, leave us alone. You have no legal rights to me. If you continue to message me, I'll have you put away again." But before sending it, she deleted it and blocked the number instead. She'd already changed her number once; she wasn't about to change it again. She understood now that it wouldn't help.

Her phone went off in her hand before she could set it down, causing her to jump.

"What can I do to help?" It was Todd.

She smiled and forgot all about Brock.

"Nothing, thanks. She's taking a bath and will most likely sleep or watch TV for the rest of the day. Sorry to miss out on today."

"I can bring some breakfast over for the caregiver. Coffee? Soup?" he suggested.

"I can't ask you to spend a full day around a sink kid."

"You're not asking. I'm offering. If it means that I can help you out and be around you, then I'm game."

She smiled and walked in to check on Simona. She sat on the edge of the bathtub before replying.

"I like my coffee with creamer and blueberry muffins from the bakery."

"Be there in fifteen," he said, before hanging up.

She leaned back as her daughter relaxed in the tub. Then she realized what he'd said. He was going to be there in fifteen minutes. She was still wearing the shorts and t-shirt she'd pulled on after removing her puked-on pajamas. Glancing at herself in the mirror, she almost cried out as she jumped up and quickly made herself more presentable for Todd's visit.

CHAPTER 12

odd had driven by the little yellow house just on the outside of town plenty of times. It sat directly on the main road and was on a triangle-shaped lot between the road that led out of town and towards his place and the road that led down to the library and the town square.

He hadn't realized she lived there until she'd sent him her address after she'd agreed to let him come over. He liked the cute cottage home. It was one of the nicest smaller places in downtown Silver Cove.

He parked just outside of the garage. He hadn't known she lived there because she parked her car in the garage.

A narrow stone pathway led into a yard with a white picket fence and to the front door. He shifted the packages of muffins, coffee, and chicken soup he'd brought along as he opened the gate and then knocked on the front door.

Olivia answered the door a moment later, her dark hair still wet from her morning shower.

"Morning." She smiled and took the coffee from him.

"Morning." He stepped in when she motioned for him to enter.

"I'm going to apologize right now about the state of the house. I'd like to blame it on the sick kid, but..." She shrugged. "Just having a kid is the real reason my house looks like this."

He smiled. "I've spent the last few days tearing out all the carpet in my place. I think I can handle a little mess from a six-year-old."

"You've been warned." She motioned for him to follow her into the living room. Simona was propped up on the sofa, watching a movie, looking a little pale. She had a mop bucket sitting next to her. "She's thrown up two more times since I took her out of the bath."

He walked over and set the soup and muffins on the kitchen countertop, which was filled with coloring books, papers, and toys. He moved over to sit next to Simona on the sofa.

"I heard you were sick?" he asked.

Simona nodded slightly. "I threw up on Mommy." He glanced over at Olivia, who sighed and nodded.

"Are you feeling any better now?" he asked Simona.

She shook her head slightly and then groaned. He saw what was going to happen before it did and thankfully managed to get the bucket under her just in time. Olivia rushed forward and started to rub her daughter's back as she mouthed, "Sorry," over her head.

When Simona was done, Olivia picked her up and disappeared down a hallway. He could hear them washing up and Simona getting sick again.

Worry for the little girl outweighed everything else in his mind. How could so much come from such a small thing?

He took the bucket to the front door where he'd seen a hose out front and rinsed it out and brought it back inside.

"Oh," Olivia said as she came out of the back. "I thought..." She shook her head and relaxed.

He smiled. "A little puke isn't going to scare me away." He held up the bucket. "It's all clean." He handed it to her. "Simona?"

"Lying in bed. She says the TV is giving her a headache." Olivia took the bucket from him.

"Should she go to the doctor or something?" he asked.

"No, she's not running a fever." She leaned against the counter. "And I received a text from Kayla letting me know that the stomach bug was going around after yesterday's event. CJ is stuck in bed today too."

"Oh," he said, glancing around.

"I'll just take this back to Simona." She started down the hallway.

He watched and waited until she returned. He could tell she was feeling slightly frazzled and embarrassed about the state of her house. But as he'd mentioned, his place currently was a wreck. He couldn't even use his kitchen, as most of the furniture from upstairs was piled in it.

The only room that was somewhat put together now was his bedroom, only because it had had hardwood floors instead of carpet in it to begin with.

When she came back out, she sat down at the table and picked up her coffee cup.

"It's probably cold now." He sat next to her. "If you want…"

"It's fine," she said after taking a sip. She grabbed a muffin from the box of sweets he'd brought along. "Mmm," she groaned. "I hadn't realized I was this hungry."

They took a moment to enjoy the muffins and the luke-warm coffee.

"If you want, I can help you clean up?" He motioned to the stack of clothes in a bucket that she'd no doubt just pulled from the dryer.

"Oh god, it's that bad, isn't it?" She moaned and laid her head on the table.

He chuckled. "Seriously, you really should see my place now. I understand not everyone can be tidy all of the time." He took her hand. "I'm just here... offering a hand if you want it."

She glanced up through her hair and sighed. "If you're offering and really want to spend time with me, then I guess you can keep me company while I fold the clothes."

"I can help..." he started to say, only to have her give him a look. "Fine." He held his hands up.

He watched her fold towels on the kitchen table and talked to her about what he was working on around his place. How he'd pulled all the furniture from each of the rooms to yank out the carpet and discovered that several rooms had amazing hardwood floors under them. He had rented a sander to clean up the floors but wasn't due to pick it up until Wednesday. Which meant he was going to be living in a disaster zone for a few more days, possibly a week, since he planned on staining and sealing the floors once he was done.

"I had these floors redone completely." She motioned to the floors.

"These are tiles, right?" He bent down and touched the wood looking tiles.

"Yes, the old wood floors in here were too far gone. Rowan, Ben, and Adam all helped me install these." She smiled. "Best decision I ever made. You can barely see dirt on them." She leaned slightly towards him. "Not that they're ever dirty."

He chuckled. "Of course not. Six-year-olds wipe their feet each time they come into the house."

He enjoyed the sound of Olivia's laughter. "I'd better check on Simona," she said once all the towels were folded.

She hoisted the laundry bucket on her hip and disappeared down the hallway.

He gathered up the empty bakery box and her empty coffee cup and looked for her trash. He found it in a massive walk-in pantry. The thing was impressive, and he stood there and tried to figure out just how and where he could build one in his house.

"Problem?" Olivia asked, directly behind him.

"No." He smiled. "This is nice. I'm trying to figure out where I can build one in my kitchen. There is only a small floor-to-ceiling cabinet. Something bigger like this would come in handy."

"What about that little closet just as you come in the back door? You could expand it." She walked over and grabbed one of Simona's papers and crayons and started drawing. He moved next to her and watched as she redesigned the main floor of his house.

She had some really good ideas, including adding a mudroom off the side porch, which would allow for a massive walk-in pantry across from it.

"You can do a built-in bench in the mudroom, you know, the kind that have cubbies under it for shoes and boots, with hooks for coats or scarfs." She continued to draw, and he could totally see what she was suggesting. "If you just build a wall right here and a doorway here"—she drew more— "it doesn't really take away from the space here." She motioned to a square he assumed was his kitchen area. He was very impressed that she remembered so much of his house. "I mean, that room was massive already." She glanced up at him. "Who needs a twenty-foot-wide entry area on the side of their house? Besides, you have the really great entry just inside your front door, with those beautiful stairs and the high ceilings." She sighed and rested her chin in her hands as if dreaming. "You'd get more use out of a mudroom and a walk-in pantry. This way, you don't touch the beautiful sunroom off the back, overlooking the water."

"I guess I need to figure out how to frame a wall." He laughed.

"You should do power, you know, have lights, outlets, and such installed as well," she suggested.

"Thanks." He sighed. "I have the guy you suggested coming to do some other electric work in a week or so. I'm afraid of what he'll say needs to be done around the place," he admitted.

"It's far better to have it done than to have a fire. This place was a fire hazard when we first moved in. Every time I turned on a light, another one flickered." She shook her head.

"I'll call tomorrow and see if he can come earlier," he agreed, knowing that he'd had problems with his toaster yesterday morning. "You're really good at this sort of thing."

She smiled. "I had to be. When we moved in here"—she shook her head— "let's just say, you're place looks a hundred times better than this one did."

He glanced around; the place looked like a home. Lived in, comfortable, and full of love. He liked her simple style of decorating and figured that, with Simona around, there couldn't be any needless trinkets or priceless items that easily broke. Unlike the home he'd grown up in. He'd never really been allowed to be a kid, to run, play, and accidentally break things.

His mother had been too refined for such antics.

Now, however, he could easily see himself living comfortably, the way he wanted, with no restraints. Now that he was finally free to decorate a space, he was finding it difficult to decide on a style.

"I'd never know. You did an amazing job," he said. Her smile grew.

"Thanks." She stood up. "I'll just go check on Simona."

He walked around the space, thinking about adding a few elements of her decorating style to his own place. She had a light, airy beach style that he liked, with a few paintings of lighthouses like the one on the end of the point he lived on. Leaning closer to one, he realized it was the same lighthouse and point. He could just make out the shape of his home and smiled.

"Like it?" Olivia said from behind him.

"I see my house." He motioned to the painting.

She chuckled. "Mine's in there too." She motioned further down and off to the side. "This place used to be blue. I had it painted yellow when we moved in."

"Where did you get this?" he asked, thinking of trying to find something similar for above his fireplace.

"There's an outdoor farmers market in town every Sunday afternoon. A local man paints them."

"I'll have to check it out." He followed her to sit on the sofa. "How's Simona?"

"Sleeping." She sighed. "I think she's drained her stomach."

"Poor thing." He leaned back and put his arm around her shoulders and pulled her closer to him, causing her to giggle.

"I'm sorry about today," she said, smiling up at him.

"This is far better than a picnic," he said, running his lips over her ear, enjoying her sexy moan as he did so. "Don't you agree?" She smelled fresh, like flowers, and tasted like sex. He couldn't wait to feel all of her under him.

"Hm." Her fingers tightened in his hair as she arched back, giving him more access to her neck.

When she tugged him down, he covered her mouth and shifted so he was over her as he took the kiss deeper. Her legs wrapped around his hips as she tugged his T-shirt up. Her fingers played over his stomach muscles.

He felt his body instantly react to her touch and desperately wanted to feel her skin next to his. She nudged him back and tugged his shirt over his head, then ran her eyes over him as he reached to start unbuttoning her blouse.

"Tell me Simona's a heavy sleeper," he said, against her lips.

She nodded. "I'm sure she will be out for a while." She pulled him back down to her.

"Should we... move into the bedroom?" he asked as he started working the buttons on her shorts.

She shook her head slightly. "No, here, just like this." She arched up while she helped him discard her shorts. Finally, she lay under him in a sexy set of blue panties and bra. "It's been too long."

His eyes ran over her perfect skin, her toned body, those perfect breasts, and moved up to her lips, full and waiting for him to kiss.

Before he discarded his jeans, he pulled out a condom that he'd thankfully shoved in his pocket that morning. When she smiled up at him, he knew that as much as he'd like to take his time enjoying their first time together, there was an urgency, a need that had to be filled.

He kissed her until he could no longer wait any longer. Her nails scraped his sides, his butt, lighting even more desires. When he pushed into her heat, she moaned his name, wrapped her arms and legs around him, and held on as he took what he wanted, gave her everything in return. Everything he'd bottled up over the years. Things he never knew he had to offer.

When they lay on the sofa, breathing heavily and wrapped around one another, he glanced at her.

"Are you all right?" he asked with a grin, since she had a large smile on her lips.

"No." She looked at him, her eyes sobering. "All right doesn't describe how I feel right now."

He chuckled and started to get up to get dressed, but she held him still.

"Just… give me a moment to enjoy this." She sighed and closed her eyes. "Do you know how long it's been since I've…"—her eyes opened— "had that."

His eyebrows shot up. "How long?"

She took a deep breath as her eyes ran over him. "Years."

He thought about it and nodded. "It's been a while for me too." She released her hold on him and he sat up and pulled on his jeans. He handed her the shirt he'd pulled from her earlier. "I'd hate to think that Simona would wake up and find us like this."

"Right." She nodded. "I should probably check on her."

"In a while." He took her hand after she'd pulled on her clothes again. "This matters," he said before rushing his lips across hers. "I don't just sleep with women and run."

"No," she agreed, "neither do I." She frowned slightly. "But I won't do anything that lets my daughter get hurt in any way. After Brock…" She paused. "The whole thing broke Simona for a while. Actually, it broke both of us. I just don't know if we can go through something like that again."

He thought about what she was saying. About what he wanted for his own life. If he could make what was between them casual.

"Is this your way of asking my intentions?" he joked.

She glanced towards the hallway and her daughter's bedroom. "This is my way of telling you I won't do anything to harm my daughter. That our relationship is more important than anything else I might want."

He nodded. "I would never expect you to choose between us. Never," he clarified.

"I believe you," she said quickly. "But sometimes the path we take leads us somewhere we hadn't planned."

He brushed a strand of her dark hair away from her face

and cupped her chin. Leaning in, he kissed her softly. "Whatever path this leads us down, I'm willing to enjoy the ride with you and with Simona."

He'd never meant any statement more in his life.

If he could enjoy the two of them for a while longer, then he was going to take that chance. Even if it meant heartbreak in the end.

CHAPTER 13

In the end, it took three days for the flu to run its course. The day after Simona had gotten sick, Olivia had spent the day in bed herself.

It had been so sweet of Todd to drop off some soup for her, though she'd left it untouched since just the smell of it caused her to rush to the bathroom.

While she'd soaked in a hot shower, Todd had entertained Simona, who was feeling much better. It warmed her heart to hear her daughter in the next room, giggling at something Todd had said or at the movie they were watching.

Todd had even helped her get Simona to bed and then stuck around and lay on the sofa with her watching a movie until she fell asleep. She hadn't heard him leave but felt him carry her to her bed and kiss her goodnight.

She'd wanted to pull him down, to snuggle up against his warm chest, but he must have known that when her daughter woke in the morning, there would be too many questions. Questions she wasn't prepared to answer at this time.

What she needed was to have a chat with Kayla and find

out just how she'd let CJ know she was dating Rowan. There were no manuals or books on how to explain to your young child that you were sleeping with a man and why.

The following day, she and Simona spent the entire time lying around the house, playing board games or watching her daughter's favorite movies. By the end of the day, she was feeling back to her normal self and decided she needed to do something to thank Todd for helping her out.

One of her favorite pastimes was baking, so, with Simona's help, she baked a large tray of brownies, the gooey triple-chocolate kind with fudge frosting and chocolate chunks and nuts all throughout. Then she became concerned that he might have a nut allergy, and she baked a second tray. She and Simona could enjoy whichever one he didn't eat.

The following day, after dropping Simona off at day care, she drove out to the point and knocked on his door.

She noticed instantly that the dark SUV was no longer parked across from his place and wondered if that was a sign that he'd found out that the message had been from Brock. She was determined not to ask him the moment he opened the door.

She didn't have to worry about that because, when he opened the door, she was distracted by the fact that he looked as green as the robe he was wearing.

"Oh no," she groaned and pushed her way into his place to feel his forehead and see if he had a fever. "Why didn't you call me and tell me it hit you too?" She set the tray of brownies on his countertop and then gasped at the destruction around his place. "You're living here? With the place like this?"

He groaned and, instead of answering, rushed from the room. She heard him close the bathroom door and sighed. She wanted to be there for him, like he'd been there for her, so she pulled out her phone and sent a text to Kayla.

"Is it okay if Simona spends the night with you? Todd's sick and I'd like to repay him for taking such good care of us when we were down."

The response was almost immediate.

"Sure, we can swing by your place and pack her some clothes after lunch."

"Thanks. I owe you one."

"Rowan and I are wanting a night away. I'll hit you up."

"Any time." She tucked her phone back in her pocket. There was a large pile of dishes in his sink, so she got to work.

He hadn't been joking—his house was a disaster at the moment. What seemed like every piece of furniture he owned was sitting in the living room and dining room.

He'd started building the wall she'd helped him come up with but hadn't gotten far. There were two-by-fours sitting in the area and some already in place, laid out where the wall would be. He had a roll of electric wire sitting with his tools along with other items he'd need to close in the section to build a mudroom and pantry.

By the time he stepped out of the bathroom, she'd cleaned his entire kitchen and had the brownies put away, since she remembered how she'd felt about any food being around her when she'd been sick.

"How are you feeling?" she asked.

He groaned and she motioned to the spot she'd cleared on his sofa.

"Rest. I've arranged for Simona to stay at Kayla's for the night." She nudged him down onto the sofa and, after putting his feet up, covered him with a blanket. "You weren't kidding when you said your place is a disaster."

He sighed. "Sorry."

"Don't be." She sat gently next to him and looked at him.

"Your color is a little better than it was when you opened the door."

"I had to go down the stairs to answer the door," he said, closing his eyes.

"I'm sorry. I should have called or texted before I came over." She glanced around and noticed that his television was sitting on the floor, unplugged. "Have any good books I can read you?" she asked.

He motioned to a stack of boxes.

"Which box?" she asked, moving over to them.

"All of them. I'm planning on building some bookcases. Just haven't figured out where yet."

She glanced around and thought about it. "Well, if you're not going to need the bedroom down here, I'd turn it into a library or reading room," she suggested.

When he didn't answer her, she glanced over and saw that he'd fallen asleep. Smiling, she walked into the other room and noticed just how large the downstairs bedroom was. It faced the front of the home yet still had an amazing view of the water across the yard. He'd emptied the bedroom of all furniture and pulled up the old carpet that had been in there.

She could just imagine two large built-in bookshelves on either side of the wide picture windows and a comfortable chair to read in sitting in front of the window.

After checking on Todd, she strolled around the rest of the house, seeing what work he'd done since the last time she'd been there.

The entire second floor looked a lot like the bedroom had. All the carpet was missing and there was no furniture left anywhere. The two bathrooms on that floor were untouched and, as she'd noticed the first time she'd walked through there, in serious need of updating.

Since he'd told her that he'd moved up to the top floor,

she avoided that area for now. She didn't want him to feel like she'd snooped around his personal space.

Heading back downstairs, she rummaged through his kitchen and found the ingredients for some homemade turkey soup. It had been a while since she'd made her grandmother's noodles, but Todd was happily snoring on the sofa, and she figured that when he woke up, he'd be ready for something to eat.

By the time Todd woke, the soup was done. She had even found a loaf of bread in the freezer and had it in the oven, making the house smell wonderful.

"I thought I dreamed that you were here," Todd said, sitting up and rubbing his hands over his face.

"How are you feeling?" she asked, handing him a glass of water. When he groaned, she said, "You need hydration."

He took the glass and sipped. "Something smells…" He frowned. "Wonderful."

"Bread and homemade turkey soup." She motioned to the kitchen. "You should be over the worst of it, since you slept for two hours."

"My stomach isn't revolting at the smell of food." He glanced down at the sweats he was wearing. "I'd like a shower first."

"You have time. Do you think you can make it upstairs by yourself?"

He smiled. "Are you asking if I want you to shower with me? Because the answer would be…" He rolled his eyes. "The answer is yes, but I'm afraid I'd need some food first for some strength to do anything other than let you wash my back."

She chuckled. "Go, shower. The food will be here when you're clean."

"And you?" he asked, before getting off the sofa.

"I have the whole night to watch over you," she answered

with a smile. "Simona's at Kayla's for the night so I can nurse you back to health, seeing as I'm the one who got you sick."

He smiled and that sexy dimple near the corner of his mouth flashed. Even though he had at least a day's worth of stubble on his chin, she could still make it out perfectly.

She busied herself by clearing off the kitchen table and setting out bowls and plates for them while he showered. She took some butter out of the fridge, added a touch of seasoning, and set it on the table.

It was a little earlier than she usually ate, but smelling the soup and bread, she knew she'd enjoy the early dinner.

When he came back downstairs dressed in clean worn jeans and a black T-shirt with his hair still damp from the shower, she figured that he was over the worse of it.

"Hungry?" she asked as she motioned for him to sit at the table.

"Starved," he said, sitting down. "It smells wonderful."

"Thanks." She set a bowl down in front of him and then went back to get the bread out of the oven where it had been warming.

"Did you make these noodles?" he asked over his shoulder. "They look homemade."

"Yes." She smiled and grabbed a bowl for herself and sat across from him. "It was my grandmother's recipe." She took a bite and smiled as he broke off a chunk of the bread and slathered it with butter.

"What's this in the butter?" he asked before taking a bite.

"Parsley, tarragon, and chervil. Along with rosemary leaves." She applied some to her own piece of bread.

"Where did you get all that? I know for a fact that I don't have any spices in my kitchen." He took another bite. "God, it's so good."

"You have them all growing just outside your door." She

motioned to the side doorway. "There's a nice herb garden out there."

He frowned. "You mean the weeds I haven't gotten around to pulling yet?"

"Don't you dare pull them." She shook her head and laughed. "I'm super jealous of your little garden. I've been trying to grow one myself, but the side of the house where I have space doesn't get enough sunlight. So, I have to settle for a smaller one inside my kitchen window."

"Okay." He nodded. "I won't tear them out. Just as long as you show me what I have and how to use them."

She laughed and agreed. After the early dinner, they headed out to the back patio to get some fresh air. They watched the water as they talked for a while. When she noticed Todd's head rolling back and his eyes grow tired again, she knew that he'd spent his energy.

"I can hook up your television so we can watch a movie?" she suggested.

He sighed. "I'm afraid I'm just not back to my normal self," he admitted as they walked inside. "The home cooking and fresh air has made me tired again."

He sat on the edge of the sofa and watched her hook up his television and the cable box.

"I have plans to hang that in the corner." He motioned to the spot.

She'd been dying to ask him about Ethan and Javan. To find out what he'd learned about the text messages. She figured if she didn't ask now, he would be asleep in a few moments.

"Did Ethan and Javan head out?" she asked, glancing over her shoulder.

"Oh, yeah, I meant to tell you. They confirmed that the text message was from the same burner phone that you received your messages from." He leaned back on the sofa and took a deep breath. "Sounds like your ex doesn't like you talking to me." He glanced over her.

She felt her heart skip. She'd been so concerned about what he'd think about a single mother, she hadn't stopped to imagine the issues Brock would bring to any future relationship she'd have. Would he break it off with her because of Brock and the threats he'd made? She hadn't realized she'd frozen in place, her entire body tense, as if waiting for something bad to happen. As if waiting for him to turn her away.

"Come here." He patted the cushion beside him.

As if hearing his voice had freed her from her fears, she moved over and sat next to him. He took her hands in his and then pulled her into a light hug.

"I can see your fear in your eyes," he said softly. "If anything, his threat, if you can call it that, makes me want to get closer to you and Simona so I can protect you both."

She relaxed and wrapped her arms around his middle. "I'm sorry he's dragged you into this."

"This?" he asked, leaning back and looking down at her. "If by that you mean this"—he brushed his lips across hers and she relaxed even more— "then there's no need to apologize. I walked willingly into… this. I'm here because I want to be here. I want you to be here. I want Simona to be part of my life, regardless."

She smiled. "She asked me if she could skip going over to Kayla's today and come over here to see you instead."

"I'm glad you're here." He pulled her back against his chest and, even though she knew he was recovering from being sick, she absolutely loved the feel of him against her.

"Olivia." Her name was a soft whisper against her ear.

"How are you feeling?" she asked, running her lips over his jaw. He'd showered but hadn't shaved, and she was finding the soft stubble sexy.

Todd leaned back and cupped her face, then placed his

lips over hers. The kiss was softer, slower, than when he'd kissed her before. Almost as if they had all the time in the world to enjoy one another.

He surprised her by standing up and lifting her into his arms.

"Todd, you're not—"

"Shh, I'm fine and you weigh next to nothing." He kissed her again and then walked towards the stairs.

By the second landing, she could tell he was a little breathless.

She smiled. "Put me down now before you fall over."

"Damn." He sighed and set her on the ground. "So much for the grand romantic gesture."

She chuckled. "Next time."

He took her hand and continued walking up the next set of stairs. She noticed instantly that he'd made the space his by moving the large bed that had been in the downstairs room up there. It sat opposite the wall of the windows so one could simply lie in bed and see the water.

There was a large gray chair in the corner of the room and what appeared to be new distressed gray nightstands and a matching dresser.

"I like what you've done with the room," she said as he pulled her into his arms. He kissed her again while his hands moved over her body, removing her clothing slowly, as if it was a dance.

She couldn't remember ever being as moved or treated as delicately as Todd was treating her now. She didn't know what she was going to do when this was over. How she was ever going to return to her normal life once he tired of her. And she knew, deep down in her gut, that he was going to tire of her. After all, everyone she'd ever loved had discarded her after a while.

CHAPTER 14

Falling asleep with Olivia in his arms was by far the best thing he'd ever felt. He'd been exhausted after the good meal and knew that if he planned on a full recovery, he needed downtime to let his body recuperate.

He hadn't planned on falling asleep before sunset though and, when he woke up shortly after one in the morning, he was slightly surprised that Olivia hadn't woken him up or left.

He lay there, after checking his bedside clock for the time, and wondered why he'd woken up in the first place. He couldn't hear anything, but still, something was off.

Gently nudging Olivia from her position lying halfway over his chest, he sat up and looked around.

He still couldn't hear anything. He almost tripped on his jeans on the floor, then pulled them on and walked over to his window to look down over the front of his house.

He could just make out Olivia's car parked out front, and then he spotted movement behind it. It took him only a moment to pull on some shoes and get a gun from the safe in his closet.

When he hit the back door, he flipped on the flood lights, knowing it would scare away whoever was messing with her car. Still, he figured it was better than confronting a possible armed burglar or, worse, her crazed ex.

He moved quickly, feeling completely in control, as he rushed down the sidewalk. He could see a dark figure running away from the back of Olivia's car. He stood in the middle of the road and watched a man of roughly six feet wearing cargo pants and a black jacket run towards the main road.

Pulling out his cell phone, he called 911 and relayed the information to the dispatcher as he looked at the destruction left behind.

When the patrol car finally arrived, Olivia was dressed and standing beside him, angrier than he'd ever seen her before. She was on the phone with her insurance agent and a tow truck, since both of her back tires had been slashed. The entire back side of her car was destroyed.

Two local officers by the names of Tom and Scott, who Olivia introduced him to, arrived and informed them that they had pulled over Eric Torre a few miles away. The man was wearing cargo pants and a black sweatshirt. He had a sledgehammer in his trunk and a large hunting knife, which was no doubt used to slit the tires.

Scott said, "He claims he was just out for a walk," Scott said. "With a sledgehammer." He chuckled. "He claims that he hasn't had any contact with Brock in weeks."

Olivia hung up with her insurance company the moment the police had arrived.

"Why does it sound like you don't believe him?" she asked Scott.

"Because I went to school with them and know for a fact that those two have remained in contact since the moment that we arrested Brock," Scott answered.

"We'll take him in, charge him with the destruction," Tom added as he handed Olivia a report. Todd had found out that Tom was the chief of police "Scott here will take some pictures of the damage for the report. I'd suggest you take some yourself for your insurance company."

Along with her tires being slashed, both of her brake lights had been broken. The sledgehammer had been used to dent in the trunk and rear side panels. The rear window and back side windows were shattered. It was as if Eric had started on the back, afraid that if get got too close to the house, he'd set off the flood lights. Which he would have, if he'd moved to the front of her car.

"Yes." Olivia sighed. "They've requested I send them some pictures."

By the time the police left, the sun was just coming up. The tow truck came an hour later and hauled her car to the local repair shop. The man who met them seemed to know Olivia well, and she explained that her car had been in for repairs a few times that winter. He even offered to take the junker off her hands instead of her paying for repairs.

"I really need to get a more reliable car. But I only drive it in town." She had shrugged. "It's not like we go far."

"Breakfast?" he asked once they were alone again.

"Most definitely," she agreed, rubbing her forehead. "I need coffee. Lots of it."

"Agreed." He took her hand, walked towards his car, and opened the door for her to get in.

As he drove through town towards the bakery, they both remained silent, and he could tell there was a lot more bothering her than the destruction of her car.

"Are you okay?" he asked as he parked in the parking lot of Sweet Expectations.

"Yes," she answered, avoiding his gaze.

He turned off the car and shifted towards her, then took

her hand. "Olivia, I can see the fear in there." He motioned towards her face, then cupped her chin and kissed her. "Remember, I'm not going anywhere. Talk to me."

"I'm not sure what to do now." She leaned back and closed her eyes. "How am I supposed to tell Simona what happened?"

He thought about it. "Don't."

She laughed. "Right."

"No, I mean it. You did mention that you needed a new car. Call the repair shop, take the man's offer, and sell your car. Then we'll head to the nearest dealer and get you a new car. One that Brock doesn't know about."

She was silent for a while, and he imagined that she was calculating if she had enough money to afford a new car.

"I suppose it won't hurt to look," she finally admitted. "After coffee."

He smiled. "Do you think Kayla can watch Simona a while longer?"

"I'll text her and let her know while I drink my second cup of coffee," she said as they walked into the bakery.

While he ate his second apple strudel, she called Kayla, who agreed to watch Simona until they returned later that evening.

By the time they left the bakery, Olivia was looking like her normal self. She even had a slight spring in her step when they walked onto the first car lot together.

He hated that the salesmen zeroed in on him when they stopped to look at a used SUV.

"You know, it would be nice to have a bigger car. My sedan was great on gas miles, but not so great when I had to drive in the snow or to get groceries," Olivia said just before the salesman approached them.

"Welcome," the man said with a huge smile. "Looking for a new car for the missus?"

"The missus," he said with a hint of sarcasm, "is looking for a new car. I'm just along for the ride." He stepped back. To the man's credit, he turned his full attention on Olivia, who asked a bunch of questions and then moved on to a newer model with fewer miles.

In the end, he followed her out the front door and drove her to another lot on the other side of town to see what options they had. Again, he stood back as she talked to a saleswoman this time.

He was impressed with the Subaru Forester she was looking at. The price was within her budget and, even though it had higher miles than he would have liked, it wasn't as bad as what she'd been looking at on the first lot.

In the end, she talked the saleswoman down a couple thousand dollars and got her to add on a year of free oil changes and tire rotations.

"Impressive," he said quietly when the saleswoman disappeared to go get the paperwork for Olivia to sign. "Next time I need a new car, I'm taking you with me."

Olivia smiled. "I'm surprisingly good at negotiations." She shrugged. "It comes with the territory of working retail."

An hour later, they walked out of the building, and Olivia held her new set of keys. The car had been cleaned and detailed while they'd waited for her paperwork to forward to the car dealer.

"So"—he smiled at her new ride— "want to take me for a ride?"

She laughed. "Sure, hop in. You can buy me lunch." She leaned up and kissed him as he laughed.

They drove to a burger place and sat out in the sun and ate lunch. The entire time her eyes were on her new car.

"I've never purchased a car before," she admitted halfway through lunch.

"What about your old car. You had to buy it at one point."

"No, Brock purchased it. He had to sign it over to me as a condition of the divorce." She tilted her head and looked at the new car. "Besides, that was old when I started driving it. This one is… newer. It has a computer and a backup camera." She smiled. "A radio that works."

He smiled. "Simona's going to love it."

She nodded and rolled her eyes. "I may have to work extra shifts to afford it…" Her smile was back. "But it's totally worth it."

He could tell that her mind was no longer on the destruction her ex had caused her. He was happy that they had taken something terrible and made it good.

"Thank you." She turned towards him. "For today. You didn't have to tag along."

He stopped her by pulling her close. "If it means spending more time with you, I'm up for whatever."

She laughed. "Good to know. You can help out next weekend when I watch Kayla's kids."

He could tell she'd meant it as a joke, but the thought of spending time with her again had him agreeing quickly.

"Sounds like fun. I'll bring the pizza and ice cream. You supply the movies and games." He smiled.

She looked at him, then shook her head. "That was a joke. You can't tell me that you want to spend a Friday night with three kids?"

"No, what I do want to do is spend a Friday night with you. If there are three kids running around, I'm game." He smiled. "I like kids. Thinking of having some of my own someday."

Her eyes turned soft just before she turned away from him.

"I'd better go pick up Simona." She stood up and walked over to a trash bin to throw away her trash.

He followed her and when she turned around, he wrapped his arms around her.

"Thank you, for last night and today. I enjoyed the soup and you." He kissed her. "I'm looking forward to Friday night." He kissed her again.

"If you really want to deal with three kids, you're welcome to come over." She wrapped her arms around his neck. "I'd appreciate the company."

He followed her all the way back into town until she turned down the street that went to Kayla and Rowan's place. Then he continued on out of town to his home.

Walking into the empty place, with everything still a mess, he felt a slight jealousy that Olivia had someone to be there all of the time.

He'd been telling the truth. He really did want kids. The fact that he was quickly approaching thirty weighed heavily on him. His biological clock was ticking, and anyone who said men didn't have a biological clock was just plain ignorant.

For the past few years, he'd been thinking a lot about having a family of his own. Kids to share in the fun of life, a wife to enjoy and to fill his bed.

The fact that Olivia's and Simona's images kept flashing in his mind when he thought of his future made him realize that, as much as he wanted to keep things light, he was already beyond that.

He'd never felt so… himself around anyone else. Especially someone he had feelings for. He didn't want to mess that up.

Even though his mother had been terrible to him, he remembered how she'd been with his father. There hadn't been a doubt in anyone's mind that they'd cared for one another. Maybe that was why she'd changed after his father's death?

Then again, his mother hadn't really given him any attention even before his father's death. His dad had been the parent he'd cared about the most. He'd believed back then that it was because he was a boy. When he'd been younger, he had always thought that if he'd been a girl, his mother would have paid more attention to him.

Todd had always sworn that he'd never be a parent like that. Whatever gender his child was, he was going to love it, no matter what.

He thought of Simona and smiled. How had the little girl filled his heart so much in such a short time? Much like her mother had wheedled her way into his heart.

Since there was so much on his mind, he figured he'd get to work building that wall Olivia had designed for him.

A few hours later, every muscle in his body ached. But the framing for the wall was complete and ready for the electrician he'd hired to come and install outlets and lighting for the two new spaces.

To the left of the back door would be the mudroom. He planned to build a bench with cubbies like Olivia had suggested. To the right of the back door sat a massive space for the new pantry. The door for that sat directly off the kitchen area.

His mind was still whirling, so he decided to start work on fixing the stairs. He'd picked up the wood planks that would replace each step and had set up his saw on the patio.

When he stepped out to start cutting the pieces, he took a moment to watch the sun sink, changing the colors of the sky.

He flipped on the porch light and got to work cutting what he would need.

When he quit for the night, he had the first set of stairs completed. It was easy work after he found the pattern for the first few steps.

He fell face-first into bed and didn't move until his phone woke him up shortly after seven the next morning.

Seeing Ethan's number, he answered quickly.

"Morning," Ethan said cheerfully.

"Morning." He sat up and ran his hand over his face. "What's up?"

"I thought you should know that they picked up Brock Coutts last night outside of Boston for a DUI," Ethan said.

"Outside of Boston? What happened with Georgia?" he asked.

"Looks like he was making his way back up there. His parole says he wasn't allowed to leave the state of Maine, so the moment he stepped foot out of the state, he was going to be picked up anyway. I figured you'd want to know that it sounds like he won't be in your way."

"Thanks," he said and glanced over at his clock. "I'll pass the news along to Olivia."

"On another topic, I've made some headway as to who might be after you and your men. I'm following a lead out of Houston," Ethan said. "I got word that there was a hit on the rental van that had been used in AJ Collin's kidnapping and Jamie Anderson's. It appears the van was found at the bottom of a ravine…"

"Get anything off of it?" he asked. He may not have been awake before, but this bit of news had him fully awake now.

"I'll let you know when we find anything out and send it on to your local PD," Ethan added. "It's a good lead," Ethan said before hanging up.

It *was* a good lead and now that Olivia's ex was locked up again, he should feel more relaxed. But as he headed downstairs for breakfast, something was eating at him that he couldn't explain.

CHAPTER 15

The rumor about Brock was going around town and since Olivia worked in a very popular place, most everyone she knew visited her at work over the next few days. Most of them, she knew, were just checking in on her. Others wanted updates on any gossip she may have.

Since most people who walked through the doors also purchased something, she didn't mind. All the foot traffic made her days go by much faster.

The rumor about what Eric had done to her car had also made its rounds. Especially since she was driving around town in her new Subaru.

Simona had been thrilled about the new car, and Olivia believed she'd kept the news about what had happened to her old car away from her daughter.

Thankfully, she had been able to sell her old car to the man who had hauled it away for more than she'd expected. She figured that if she was able to add one more workday a month, she'd pay the car off a full year earlier than expected.

She hated being in debt. Thankfully, she wasn't the kind

of person to rack up credit card debt, so her house and car were all she owed on.

Brock had always applied for every credit card he could. Then, within months of getting the cards, he'd max them out. When they'd been married, most of her paychecks had gone to paying them each month.

She'd lucked out during the divorce since all of the credit cards had been in his name and not hers. She'd also been lucky when the judge had decided to make the debt Brock's responsibility due to the circumstances and Brock had been stuck with the payments instead of her. She'd been happy to hand over all of Brock's debts to Bethany since she knew he wouldn't be paying any of it himself.

Shortly after Brock and Bethany had separated, she'd found out that he'd learned that lesson of having things in his name and, during their short relationship, had maxed out several of Bethany's credit cards. Word was floating around that Bethany had to file bankruptcy shortly after she'd dumped Brock.

It was hard to stop herself from comparing Todd to Brock. During empty moments in her workday, those comparisons deepened into every aspect of her knowledge of both men.

The physical differences between the men were obvious —Brock was shorter and bulkier. Todd was tall, lean, and full of sexy muscles the likes of which Olivia had never gotten to enjoy before.

Todd seemed far more organized than Brock had ever been in the years she'd known him.

They were night and day, even when it came to how the men had dealt with Simona. Sure, Brock had been an average father and, to her knowledge, he'd never harmed Simona. But the way he'd talked to their daughter was proof that he'd never fully loved her either.

She'd been... a thing. Something he could use to get attention. After the divorce, Brock had used their daughter as a prop to get women. He'd even gloated about it on several occasions.

"I've got so many women lined up to be with me," Brock had said one evening when he'd dropped Simona off. "They all want to sleep with me. Too bad you're missing out. Who would want you now that you look the way you do?" He'd meant her stretch marks from giving birth. She had tried everything to hide them from Brock after Simona had been born. But he'd noticed them. He'd noticed every single one of her imperfections. He'd made fun of her for each and every one of them their entire time together.

At one point, she'd tried to fight back, to point out the fact that he'd been gaining weight, getting a beer gut, but that had turned out worse. He'd bent her fingers back, twisted her wrist until she'd believed it would snap, then slapped her until she'd almost blacked out.

She'd never mentioned any of his imperfections again, even after they were divorced.

There had been so much that she couldn't do around Brock. For years she'd felt like her true self had just... disappeared.

How long had it taken her to feel like she could be herself again? Until she'd felt like she was free to purchase items without asking for permission.

Even simple little things like spending money on groceries had caused guilt for the first year after the divorce. Then Brock had started embedding himself in their life again, and she'd sank back into her old ways.

So much of who she was was because of how he'd treated her. Now that she was free of all that, she didn't want that to happen again. No way did she want to feel like anyone was in control of her or her daughter. Never again.

It was one of the reasons she wanted to keep things casual between her and Todd. She'd trusted before and had paid the price for it.

At least now Brock was locked up and, if the rumors were true, he wasn't going to be getting out anytime soon. He'd not only broken the terms of his parole, but he'd broken the law and, according to one report, had caused an accident.

There was no way he was going to be in her or Simona's life for a while now. They were safe once again.

She was slightly surprised to see Todd come in one afternoon for a massage. Since she was busy with a customer, he smiled at her, held up a bundle of purple flowers and made a show of setting them on the counter for her, then waved as he headed to the back room.

After the customer left with their purchases, she walked over and buried her face in the flowers as she glanced over the appointment books to see that he was marked down for two massages that week.

This was twice now that he'd gotten her flowers. If she wasn't careful, she could become used to it.

When he came out of the back room, he walked directly over to her and wrapped her in his arms.

"Thanks for the flowers," she said as she held onto him.

"I saw them and thought of you. Now I feel one hundred percent." He kissed her.

She smiled. "Problems?"

"I've been working on the flooring, which means a lot of hours bent over." He stretched his back. "The massages help."

"Yoga would help even more," she suggested. "Tomorrow morning, I'll be here in yoga pants." She smiled.

"You make a very compelling argument." He pulled her back into his arms. "What time do you get off work?"

She glanced down at her watch. "Half an hour. Kayla's

going to bring Simona by, and we were going to grab some pizza."

"Care if I tag along?" he asked, making her smile.

"We'd love it."

"Good. Until then, I have some stocking up to do. I'm supposed to get…" He pulled out a slip of paper from his pocket. "Some oils and lotions to help with my soreness."

She took the paper from him and walked over to grab what he needed while he shopped for other items.

By the time she was done checking out all of his items, Amy was there to take over the store.

Kayla walked in a few moments later, looking a little flustered.

"Sorry," she said quickly. "I've been running late all day." She rolled her eyes.

Olivia scooped up Simona in a hug and kissed her.

"How's my girl?" she asked her daughter. Simona's dark locks were messy and falling out of the braid she'd done earlier that morning.

"Good." Simona pushed her away and then ran over to Todd, who was there to scoop her up for a hug. "Can Todd come with us for pizza?" she asked.

"Maybe you can ask Todd?" Olivia said with a smile.

"Can you?" She turned her face to his.

"Pizza?" he asked, his voice low as if he was thinking about it. "What kind of pizza?"

Simona giggled. "With pepperoni and olives." She leaned closer to him and lowered her voice. "My favorite."

He smiled. "Mine too. I guess I can tag along then."

She had never had as much fun eating pizza before. Todd seemed to love to entertain them both with stories of his childhood or places he'd traveled to.

"So, that's why you should never climb to the top of a pyramid," Todd said, finishing up his latest story. The pizza was gone, and Simona had been eagerly listening to him, but Olivia could see that her daughter was growing very tired and knew that bedtime was quickly approaching.

"There really aren't mummies, are there?" Simona asked.

"There are, but they don't walk around like in *Scooby Doo*," Todd answered.

Simona's eyes grew wide. "You watch *Scooby Doo*?"

Todd chuckled. "Who doesn't? Saturday morning cartoons are still my favorite." Todd winked at Olivia and she smiled. She highly doubted the man sat down and watched cartoons, any time of the day.

In her house, they were usually going at all times of the day when Simona was around. Not that she let her daughter watch television that much. Half the time Simona wasn't even in the room. She lost interest in them often and would head to her bedroom to play.

She'd tried, at first, to be one of those parents that had limited her daughter's television time. But as a single parent, life was so hectic that, half the time, she was right there with her daughter, relaxing.

She always planned fun outings for the two of them on her days off. They often went hiking, to the beach, or on playdates with friends.

Next year, she was determined to have Simona start dance or a team sport, whatever her daughter showed interest in. She knew in the end it would make her life more hectic, but she didn't mind.

As Todd continued to talk, Simona climbed up into his lap and fell asleep.

Todd acted like it was the most normal thing in the world to be holding Simona. She knew that the two had grown close last week when she'd been sick.

Simona liked Todd. That much was fact. She was almost infatuated with him. When they were alone at home, she would often ask her if they could call and invite him over for dinner or to watch movies.

Each time she'd made the excuse that he was busy fixing up his house.

Simona had even asked Todd before their pizza had arrived if he was done fixing his house yet. As she explained it, she wanted more time to hang out with him.

Even her daughter enjoyed his company. How was she supposed to fight against falling deeper in the hole when everything was against her?

The only way she could avoid becoming too attached was to remind herself how Brock had changed. That thought kept her grounded. Not that she truly believed Todd would change from who he was. She knew that all men weren't bad. She was surrounded by plenty of good men every single day.

After pizza, the three of them walked down the street to the pier. When her daughter grew tired, she lifted her into her arms to carry her, only to have Todd reach over and easily take her into his arms.

Instantly, Simona laid her head on his shoulder as if it was the most natural thing in the world to do.

"She's getting so big," Olivia said when they stopped at the end of the dock. She'd noticed that her daughter's legs went down to just below Todd's knees. "How did she get so big so quickly?" she asked, seeing that her daughter was fast asleep.

"That's what kids are supposed to do," Todd said with a smile. He reached over and took her hand in his free one. It would have taken both of her arms and hands to keep Simona up, not to mention her back would have been hurting by now under her daughter's weight. Todd, however, acted like Simona weighed next to nothing.

"I suppose," she said, wishing for years and years of her daughter being just the way she was now. "Soon she'll start looking at boys, stop wanting to hang out with me as much." She leaned on the railing and looked out over the water.

It was easily her favorite time of the day. The sun was just setting, leaving the water growing darker while the sky filled with shades of every color. All the boats were back in their spots for the night, tucked in until they left again just before dawn for another day of fishing or excursions.

"I'm thinking there is already one boy she's crazy about," Todd said softly.

She turned towards them, smiling at her daughter's dark hair falling over her face. "She does seem to like you."

He chuckled. "I was talking about CJ."

Olivia frowned. "What?"

Todd's laughter continued. "You should see the fear in your eyes." He shifted Simona slightly. "He was all she could talk about over dinner and the other day when I watched her when you were sick."

Olivia relaxed slightly. "They're friends."

"It's more than that. She has other friends she doesn't talk this much about. Besides, it's not that, it's what she says about him." He reached up and brushed a hand down Simona's hair, soothing it. The gentle way he treated her daughter had her heart melting. "From what she says, she can't stand him one minute and, the next, she's telling you something cool CJ did." He nodded slightly. "That's infatuation."

Olivia thought about it. Really thought for a moment. Simona did talk about CJ a lot. She'd just believed it was because they were so close. They were like brother and sister.

Then slowly, she started seeing it the way Todd saw it, and she realized he was telling the truth. Simona liked CJ. *Liked* liked.

Her shoulders sank and she turned away from the water

to lean back on the railing. What was she going to do now? How was she going to let her little girl go?

"Hey." Todd took her hand again, shifting the sleeping Simona so he could move closer to her. "It's not like she's moving in with the kid tomorrow. So, your daughter has her first crush." He smiled. "How old were you when a boy caught your eye for the first time?"

She thought about it and realized she had been Simona's age.

"See." Todd squeezed her hand and then dropped it to get a better hold on Simona. "Did you run away from your parents' house and get married when you were seven or eight?"

She chuckled. "No, of course not."

Todd smiled. "Then I'd say you have nothing to worry about. At least for another…"—he narrowed his eyes— "eight years."

Her smile fell away again, and she felt her stomach drop.

"Ten," he jumped in quickly. "Or twelve," he offered, and she knew he was just trying to make her feel better. "Years and years from now." He pulled her close to his side, and she wrapped her arms around him and her daughter.

"I never want to let go," she said, resting her face next to Simona's.

"Then I'll hold on forever," Todd said softly as he kissed the top of her head.

It hadn't been what she'd meant, but just hearing it, she realized how wonderful it sounded. How much she could get used to being held. Being guarded, protected, and cherished.

If she let her guard down, she could just imagine letting Todd consume her life like Brock had.

She pulled back, took a step away, and wrapped her arms around herself. "I'd… better get her home and in bed." She reached for Simona, but Todd shook his head. "I'll carry her back to your car." He shifted Simona again, who remained asleep even when he gently set her in her car seat and buckled her in.

After shutting the car door, he turned to her, wrapped his arms around her, and kissed her until she relaxed and completely forgot why it was a bad idea to let him in.

Her body wanted to be with him more than anything, but as she drove home, her mind and heart knew that there was no way she should chance it. Not again. She knew that it was only a matter of time before she'd have to break things off with him.

If she was going to survive, she knew the day was coming when she'd have to be completely alone again. After all, she'd convinced herself that it was for the best. It was for the benefit of her and Simona.

They'd been alone for years now and things had been just fine.

But, as she tucked her daughter into bed, she knew that it was a lie. There was no way she was going to be okay, not now that she'd gotten a taste of life with Todd by her side.

Once she'd tasted how sweet life could be with a man who was kind and generous next to her, she doubted she could ever convince herself that she was better off without him.

CHAPTER 16

Todd could tell that something had changed with Olivia. Whenever he texted or called and suggested they get together, she had some excuse as to why they couldn't.

When Friday finally rolled around, he showed up on her doorstep, flowers, pizzas, and fixings for ice cream sundaes in hand, without waiting for a formal invitation.

He could hear the rowdiness of the kids inside the house before Olivia answered the door. He smiled and then laughed when he noticed her T-shirt was completely soaking wet, along with her hair and half of her shorts.

"Having a water fight?" he asked cheerfully, holding out the flowers for her.

"No, my sink just broke." She left him standing at the door as she raced back inside.

Following her, he gasped when he noticed a full spray of water shooting into the air from her kitchen sink.

Setting the flowers, pizzas, and other groceries down, he rushed over to help her turn off the water.

By the time she crawled out from under the sink cabinet, she was completely soaking wet. His eyes instantly went to her perfect nipples poking out of her soaked shirt.

"Um…" He glanced over at the kids, who were sitting on the sofa, watching the entire scene unfold. "Why don't you go change into some dry clothes while I feed the kids?"

Olivia looked down at her shirt and then gasped as she pulled the wet material away from her body. "I'll… yes," she said, her face turning red as she rushed from the room.

"Todd!" Simona rushed to him and jumped up into his arms. "You're here. Mommy said you couldn't come." He hugged her and then watched her bottom lip jut out in a cute little pout.

"I'm here now," he said easily. "I brought some pizza and ice cream."

"Ice cream," all three kids shouted. CJ and Willow started jumping up and down on the sofa while Simona squirmed in his arms. Setting her down, he moved over and put the ice cream away in the freezer and started getting out the kids' plastic plates and dishing them each a slice.

When Olivia came out of her bedroom, changed into a pair of yoga pants and a sweatshirt with her hair pulled back into a short ponytail, all three of the kids were sitting at the table, eating pizza and drinking milk he'd poured them in child cups. He'd found a pretty blue vase to put the flowers he'd gotten for her in, and she stopped to bury her face in them and breathe in their scent.

"Thank you for these." She touched the soft pink petals. Then she looked around as if she was surprised that they weren't throwing pizza at one another.

"Come, sit down." He held up a plate with a slice of pizza on it, then set it down at the head of the table. When she approached him, he pulled the glass of wine he'd poured for her out from behind his back and held it out for her.

Her eyes narrowed, and she took a deep breath before taking the wine from him. He could tell there was something wrong but figured he would wait until the kids were asleep before he asked her about it.

For the next two hours, he was more entertained than he had been in years. Watching Simona interact with CJ and Willow assured him that three kids, two girls and one boy, was the perfect dynamic for a family.

CJ clung to him and listened to his Army stories, while Simona and Willow played together or watched a movie.

Olivia, now that she was dry and didn't have to focus solely on the kids, had pulled out a toolbox and was working on fixing the sink.

Since he knew that she probably knew more about it than he did, he worked on keeping the kids out from under her feet.

Once she had the sink working again, he helped each kid create their very own sundae before making his own.

"I see you're a toffee lover." He motioned to Olivia's sundae. She'd topped it with the toffee chunks he'd brought along. In truth, he might have gone a little crazy in the candy aisle. There were bags of almost every kind of candy and topping.

Still, the kids had enjoyed it and put a little of each on their choice of ice cream.

"Toffee." She shrugged. "If I could, I'd put it everywhere." She smiled and took a bite. "You…" She motioned with her spoon. "Oreos?"

"When I was in high school, I could eat an entire bag of them myself."

Her eyebrows went up. "You weren't a chubby kid?"

He laughed. "No, just a skinny kid with a very high metabolism. Now"—he patted his flat stomach and leaned back, knowing he'd hit top— "I have to hit the gym a dozen times a week to work off one Oreo."

She smiled and glanced over to where the kids were finishing up with their sundaes, sitting at the bar countertop. "After Simona, my entire diet had to change. Anything with too much sugar, and I pay for it in the gym."

He nodded as his eyes ran slowly over her. "I'd say it's working. You'll hear no complaints from me. Even if you gain a little extra." He reached out and laid his hand on her thigh. "I like soft." He squeezed gently. "Any way that you are, I think I'd enjoy you."

Olivia's eyes darted to the kids and then back to his. "Todd, we—"

"Later," he said smoothly, knowing where she was heading and understanding that they didn't have the privacy to talk about it now.

Olivia nodded and stood up to gather the dishes. While the kids played an impromptu game of hide-and-seek in the house, he helped her wash them. Then the kids were shuffled into the bathroom to clean up. While Willow and Simona took a bath together, CJ opted for a shower in the guest bathroom and was determined to get himself ready for bed.

Once everyone was clean and wearing their pajamas, they sat on the sofa to watch one last show together before they all went into Simona's room and settled down for the night.

Taking Olivia's hand, he shut Simona's bedroom door gently, so as to not wake any of the kids, and pulled her out into the living room.

He tugged her down to sit next to him on the sofa and turned to her.

"So, are you wanting to break things off?" he asked easily.

She seemed a little taken back, but then relaxed back and sighed.

"No, it's just... I can't promise you that this will go any further. I..." She shook her head and avoided his eyes. "It's just not possible."

"Oh?" he asked, feeling relieved that at least she wasn't breaking it off with him. He wanted more time with her and Simona. Time to explore what he was feeling for the pair of them.

Olivia's eyes darted to his. "I don't think I'll ever allow myself to have what others have."

He thought about her statement. Ran it over a few times in his head. "Allow yourself to have what others have? You mean happiness?"

She sighed and nodded. "Yes, I suppose if you think of it that way."

"So, no more kids?" he asked. He saw sadness fill her eyes. "I mean, sure, I'd hoped, but... if it means..." She shook her head. "I suppose not."

He held in a chuckle. "Okay, then, just because you married an ass once, you think you're destined to do it again?"

She swallowed and avoided his eyes again. "I can't take that chance. Not with Simona. I'm responsible—"

"Bullshit," he said softly. She looked at him, and he saw fear behind those silver eyes. He mentally kicked himself for causing it, but then realized that if he wanted more with her, she had to understand, to know that he was nothing like Brock.

He took her hand in his and pulled it up to his lips. "Olivia, I will never raise my hand to you or Simona in anger. That doesn't mean"—he met her eyes— "that I don't occasionally raise my voice. Understand?"

She nodded slowly. "I just don't think I can handle another broken heart."

He felt his heart break slightly at her meaning. Had she really loved Brock that much? Maybe she still did? Is that why she was avoiding the next level with him? What was the next level?

"Can we just..." She looked into his eyes. "Take things slower?"

He wanted to answer no, but looking deep into her eyes, he knew that if he did, he could lose her. So instead, he nodded and pulled her close, then kissed her gently until he felt that if he didn't leave now, he wouldn't be able to. Pulling away was one of the hardest things he'd done in a long time.

"I'll let you get some rest." He stood up. "Thanks for tonight." He started towards the door.

"Todd?" She stopped him; his hand was on the doorknob. "Thank you for understanding." He nodded quickly and then left.

For the next two weeks, he did what she'd asked. He backed off as much as he could. It wasn't as hard as he thought it would be since he had so much work at the house to keep him busy. Both the electrician and the plumber had come out and spent more than a week each repairing or replacing what needed to be fixed.

He'd taken a few breaks and had joined Olivia for Thursday morning yoga classes. He figured one day a week was all he could handle, especially when he walked away more sore than he had been when he'd replaced the flooring.

He'd also had dinner with Olivia and Simona on three occasions. Each time, he'd returned home alone with nothing but a few stolen kisses to keep him satisfied.

When he'd finished replacing all of the flooring in his house and had painted all the rooms, he decided that he didn't want to put back any of the old furniture. Instead, he sent Olivia a text message asking her to go along with him on her next day off to scour through the furniture stores for items that would fit the new space better.

When she agreed, he counted it as a small victory. Spending time alone with him hadn't been something she'd agreed to since their talk.

When the shopping day arrived, she picked him up and drove into the city while they chatted casually and caught up with each other's lives.

"So, what furniture are you looking for?" she asked him when they parked at the first store.

"Basically everything to fill the house," he answered with a chuckle. "My mother purchased the stuff currently in the house. I'd like to get rid of everything."

"Everything?" Her dark eyebrows shot up.

"Yeah," he agreed. "It's all outdated and some of it is even falling apart."

"Okay, so…" He saw she was thinking about it. "Four bedrooms' worth of furniture?"

"Four bedrooms, a dining room, and an office. "And if I'm going to redo the loft above the garage, I'll need to come up with stuff for up there as well. But that can come later. For now, four bedrooms, an office, and a dining room."

"Easy enough," she said, and he followed her into the furniture store.

Three hours and several thousand dollars later, they walked out of the third furniture store with everything he needed to fill the home purchased and scheduled for delivery.

"I don't know how you did it," he said, opening her car door for her. "You're simply amazing." He kissed her before letting her climb into the driver seat.

They had been an incredible team when it came to shopping. At first, he hadn't known what sort of items he wanted to put in his home. He'd looked at several assorted styles until he finally found the style he liked best. He would continue the beach vibe with soft grays and beechwoods with light blue accents.

Light and airy was how Olivia described it. "The perfect beach vibe, and comfortable and homey. Not too feminine and not to bland," she'd said, which he had taken as a good sign, so he'd stuck with it.

"I've never been called amazing because of my shopping skills before," Olivia joked as she started the car.

"How about we get some food?" he suggested.

"I could eat."

"Know of any good places around here?"

"Several. It depends on what you're in the mood for," she said as she started to drive.

His mind instantly jumped to his desire for her. How he'd missed touching her, tasting her, being with her. Not just in the physical sense, but in the whole. Everything about her. He wanted to laugh with her and not have this... bubble between them.

When she pulled in at a Thai place, he glanced over at her. "Thai It Up?" He chuckled at the name of the restaurant.

She looked over at him. "Is this okay? It's not often I get to indulge."

"I love Thai. It's just... I didn't think there were any good places around," he said as he got out of the car.

"This is it. The only good place within fifty miles," she said as he took her hand and walked towards the door.

"Then we'll have to come into the city more often." He opened the front door for her.

The woman behind the counter smiled. "Welcome back, Miss Olivia."

"Thanks, Malee. This is Todd," Olivia said as the woman showed them to a booth.

"Mr. Todd, welcome," Malee said as she motioned to the booth. "This okay?"

"Yes, thanks, Malee. How is Sunan? How was his first year in college?" Olivia asked as they sat down.

"Oh, he did good. All A's." Malee's smile grew. "So proud."

"Is he back for the summer?" Olivia asked.

"No, his first summer, he is taking classes still. He wants to get ahead." The woman poured them each a glass of water.

"Sunan is going to Harvard," Olivia told him. "He's sixteen."

"Wow." Todd smiled. "You must be proud."

"So proud." The woman smiled. "You look over the menu now." She went to help other customers who had walked in.

By the time they ordered their food, the entire restaurant had filled up.

"The food must be good here," Todd said, looking around.

"The best," Olivia agreed.

He took a deep breath. "So, I've been thinking."

"Okay." She took a sip of her water. "About?"

"Us." He reached across and took her free hand. "I know you wanted things to go slower." He felt her tense in his hand. "And I'm okay with that," he added quickly. "But I do have a few of my own stipulations." She relaxed and nodded.

"Okay," she said slowly.

He looked into her eyes. "One, I'd like a scheduled date night."

She smiled. "I think that can be arranged."

"One for just us, and one night a week with the three of us," he added. He felt her tense again. "Simona is part of you, part of your life. I'd like a chance to know all of you. Besides…" He smiled. "She brings me joy. I like hanging out with her."

Olivia was quiet for a moment, then nodded. "Okay, two nights a week. But, just to warn you, your time with Simona may just be watching cartoons or playing games at our house."

His smile grew. "Perfect."

"Any other stipulations?" she asked.

He ran his thumb over her palm slowly. "We pick back up where we were, physically. I miss being with you." He watched her eyes heat with desire. "And I think you miss it as well."

CHAPTER 17

What was she supposed to do? How was she supposed to deny something that was true, deep down? She missed him. She was torn between protecting her and Simona's hearts and wanting to leap and enjoy her feelings again.

"See, you can't deny it," Todd said easily with a smile. "I've seen how you react when I touch you."

His thumb was running over her palm, the simple touch already lighting fires deep within her.

"I can't deny it," she admitted. "But part of me is afraid."

"Of?" he asked. His thumb stopped moving. "Me?"

"No," she answered quickly. "Of my feelings. I don't think I could bear letting go. Trusting again."

This wasn't the time or the place she'd hoped to have this conversation. Not that she'd ever planned on telling him about her fears, but certainly not in Thai It Up.

He was silent for a while then nodded. "The last person I opened up to was when I was on assignment. She was the daughter of a diplomat. I believed that Kimber could see past my assignment, so when she found out what I was, I told her everything. Well, almost everything. I had naively believed that she didn't know what her father was doing. How he was silently locking up and murdering his countrymen and women all in the name of purification, money, and power." He leaned back, dropping his hand from hers and, for the first time, she noticed weariness in his eyes. Weariness and something else she couldn't pinpoint. "When I told her that I was on a mission, she at first acted like she didn't know about her father. Then, New Year's Eve, during a large party her father was throwing, I was attacked."

"What happened?" Worry caused her to lean forward, even though he was safe, sitting across from her.

"Kimber had told her father everything. She stood over me, even helped while her father's men beat me, tied me up, and then took me away to kill."

"How did you escape?" she asked, eager to hear the rest of the story.

"Thankfully, I was wearing a wire. My team swooped in the first moment they could and rescued me. If it wasn't for them, I would have been dead a long time ago," he admitted. "So, I understand how hard it is to trust again after being betrayed. Brock betrayed you and Simona. I won't." He took her hand again. "This is my promise."

She believed him. Deep down, she knew that if anything was going to go wrong between them, it wasn't going to be because of betrayal. Not in the sense that Brock had betrayed her.

On the drive home, she thought about everything he'd told her. Everything he'd confided in her. Wasn't it her turn to open up?

He hadn't prodded or asked her what had happened, but she knew that it was time to let him in. So when she pulled into his driveway, she turned off the car and turned to him.

"I'd like to come in," she said softly.

Instead of answering, he pulled her close and kissed her. She melted against him, letting her entire body react instantly to his closeness. To the hardness of his arms and chest against her own.

It felt too good, being held again. Held by someone who cared. Someone who understood how difficult it was for her to open up. To trust.

When he pulled away, she knew that it was pointless hiding anything from him. If he didn't already know the details, he could guess what she'd been through.

When they stepped into his house, she turned to him.

"Maybe a glass of wine?" she asked.

He nodded and she followed him into the kitchen.

He'd gotten so much done since the last time she'd been inside. The wall separating the mudroom and pantry was done and it looked like it had always been part of the house. He even had a large, framed picture of the sea hanging on it. The hutch that she'd helped him pick out sat on the wall in the dining area. Even though it was empty of anything, it made the space feel complete and matched his oak dining table and chairs almost perfectly.

His living room was back to normal, with his television hanging up just to the left of the fireplace.

She walked down the hallway and glanced into the room that used to be his bedroom and noticed it was now the reading room she'd suggested.

Brand new bookshelves sat on either side of the wide windows. She walked over and ran a finger over the edges of a few books that sat on the shelves he'd painted a sky blue and noticed he'd organized them by author.

"You have an impressive collection," she said over her shoulder.

"I like to go to book conventions and author signings," he said from the doorway. "I started when I was in England for a few months and, well, I guess I never stopped." He chuckled. "There's one in two weeks in Boston I plan on going to. More than a dozen of my favorite authors will be there."

"Really?" She turned around, and he held up two glasses of red wine. "Care for some company?"

He smiled as he handed her the glass. "I purchased two tickets in hopes that I could convince you to come along for the weekend."

She nodded. "I'll see if Crystal or Kayla can take Simona." She sipped the wine. The dryness and bite of it instantly gave her the strength she needed.

Walking back out to the living room, she sat down on the sofa and motioned for him to sit next to her.

"I quit college to marry Brock," she said, looking down into the dark red liquid. "I was twenty years old and had never felt like anyone had ever loved me. My parents tolerated me and expected me to disappear after I came of age. When Brock swooped in with his sweet words and promises, I figured the rest would just come naturally."

"It didn't," Todd said.

"No," she agreed. "A few months later, we married at the courthouse. He didn't have the money for a big wedding, and my parents… well, they weren't going to pay for anything. Not since they'd put all their money into the first two years of community college. Money they deemed wasted since I was no longer going to be going to school." She took another sip of the wine. "Shortly after marrying, Brock convinced me that we should move to Silver Cove. His hometown. The best decision, in hindsight. We moved into a small apartment above his parents' garage until they moved further south after his father retired." She glanced up at him. "They're in the Keys now. Anyway, three months after they left, and we moved into a one-bedroom trailer at the trailer park, I gave birth to Simona. Less than a month after giving birth, we got in a fight over diapers. Brock felt everything to do with Simona was too expensive since it was eating into his drinking money. When he hit me, it didn't register with me at first." She reached up and touched her cheek, somehow still remembering the burn. The physical pain was long gone but never forgotten. "I packed our bags, put Simona in her carrier, and had every intention of leaving, but Brock talked me out of it. After all, I had nowhere to go. At that point, I didn't have a job or money of my own. Then it became a standard once-a-month fight, which then turned into twice a month, then progressed to once a week until, suddenly, it was a daily event."

"What made you finally leave?" he asked as he got up and poured her more wine. She hadn't realized she'd gone through the entire glass and set it down, needing a breath.

"Brock left. He was having an affair with a coworker," she admitted. She no longer felt or cared about the sting from the betrayal.

"How long did that last?" Todd asked.

"A few months. Then he was back knocking on my door, wanting to get back together. I was working at that point, and he was still working nights at Walmart. He was desperate to control someone. Somehow, he started back in on me, without my knowledge. I was stupid to let him have any control over me."

"He broke your arm after you were divorced?" he asked.

"Yes. We'd argued about me filling in for Kayla the night that Willow was born." She glanced down at the pale white scars on her wrist. "I went to work and passed out. Rowan found me on the floor and called the police to have Brock taken in. They, my friends, convinced me to press charges finally. Throughout it all, they were right there for me and Simona."

"They do seem like a pretty amazing group. I still can't

believe that Sarah and Crystal remember me," Todd said, setting his glass down and taking her hand in his. His fingers played over the small scars, then he lifted her wrist to his lips and brushed a kiss over the spot gently, making her heart melt.

"How was I to know that family could be like that?" She felt tears sting her eyes. "There is no place I'd rather be than here. I want Simona to grow up knowing what love is. Feeling it from not only me, but everyone else around her."

"Of course, you do," he said softly.

"So, you see why I'm concerned. If you…" She shook her head. "I can't ask you to stay. To commit to a life here. Not when you've been so many other places."

"Hey." He lifted her chin with his fingers until they were eye to eye. "Have I given you the impression that I'm going anywhere?"

"You… told Sarah that you might fix the place up and sell it."

He frowned. "When?"

"The first night we met."

He shocked her by laughing. "If I ever had that intention, it disappeared the moment I kissed you." He pulled her close. "Trust me, I'm not going anywhere soon. I've put sweat and blood"—he showed her a few knicks on his hands and smiled — "into making this my home." She relaxed. "Is that all that was holding you back?" he asked.

She thought about it. "That and my fears about trusting again," she admitted. "But after your story, I'm willing to chance it. For you." She lifted her hand and ran her fingertips over his face. "You've let your beard grow."

He smiled. "It's the style. Besides, you said you liked it."

"I do." She leaned in to kiss him. The feel of it brushing against her face warmed her.

"Olivia, I want you," he said softly. "I know you said…"

"I want you too. Take me upstairs." She looked into his eyes.

Then he was kissing her, and she no longer cared where they were, if they went up to bed or not. All that mattered was him. His hands ran slowly over her body, causing her to burn. She wrapped her legs around his hips, pushing his erection, still trapped in his jeans, up against her core. She wanted him, needed him, inside her.

It was a craving so deep, so primitive, that her mind simply stopped working, allowing her body to take over. She clawed at him, pulling, pushing his clothes from his body while he did the same to her.

When she finally felt his skin against hers, she moaned and sighed as her body continued to build. Her nails scraped his skin, her fingers dug into his muscles, his hips, pulling him until finally he settled between her thighs.

His lips roamed over her jaw, her neck, her breasts as she waited in anticipation for him to thrust into her. When he finally did, she cried out his name, trying to hold onto that moment forever, needing it to last. Willing it to stay a lifetime or longer.

Then he started moving inside her, and the last threads holding her heart tucked away snapped.

When she fell asleep in his arms on the sofa, wrapped in his embrace, she knew that she was helplessly in love and there would be no recovering from heartbreak this time.

Her phone alarm chimed almost an hour later, signaling that she needed to go get Simona from Kayla's house.

"Hmm." Todd moaned and buried his face further into her hair.

"I have to go get Simona," she said, trying to untangle their limbs.

"Mkay, bring her back here. I want to hold you all night long," Todd said, his voice deep with sleep.

"I… wish I could, but not this time." She pulled out of his hold and slipped on her jeans and shirt.

"What do you need to make this place more comfortable for her so we can have sleepovers?" Todd asked, fully awake now and sitting up, watching her.

She thought about it. "Simona would need a bedroom and maybe some of her things. Not to mention an explanation of why we were sleeping over."

He cringed. "You want to tell your six-year-old what we're doing?"

"No." She rolled her eyes. "But she should know that you and I… that we are dating, at least."

"You don't think she knows that already?"

She shrugged, unsure what her daughter thought about their relationship. "I need to talk to her."

"Yeah." He smiled and walked over to her, then wrapped her in a naked embrace, though she was fully clothed. "Go, have a good night. But next time you come over, plan on staying. Both of you." He kissed her.

"Okay," she finally agreed, before turning away from him and leaving. If she hadn't left then, she doubted she would have been able to. He was warm and it felt so good to be held by someone she cared for. Someone she loved. Completely.

When she walked into Kayla's house ten minutes later, there was a blanket fortress in the living area and all three kids were taking turns jumping from the back of the sofa onto the pile of sofa cushions.

"Just in time," Kayla said with a smile.

"Looks like you guys have been having fun," Olivia said as Simona rushed over to give her a hug.

"I can jump higher than CJ," Simona said loudly.

"No, you can't," CJ countered. He proceeded to climb up and jump off the back of the sofa in a great show. "See!" he said as if his actions were all the proof he needed.

"I jumped higher than that," Simona screamed, rushing over to show him and the room.

Kayla rolled her eyes. "This has been going on for half an hour. They actually wanted me to judge who was higher." She leaned in. "Don't fall for it. You can't win, no matter who you pick."

Olivia chuckled. "Thanks for watching Simona again."

Kayla smiled as she ran her eyes over her face. "I see you had a good time." She wiggled her eyebrows. "Your hair is messed up and your shirt is on backwards. Must have been a real good time."

"It is not…" She started to deny it, but then she looked down and groaned when she noticed her shirt was indeed on backwards, which only caused Kayla to laugh.

"Oh, trust me, I know how it is. Those first few months of seeing someone." Kayla's smile turned wishful. "With Rowan, every day feels like the first few months."

She wondered if she would always feel this way with Todd. Somehow, she knew that she would.

Kayla turned back to her with a smile. "Yeah." Her friend pointed to her face. "That's the smile, that right there is what bliss looks like." Kayla surprised her by wrapping her arms around her. "I'm glad you finally found it. You deserve happiness."

That night, Olivia lay in bed replaying the day's event. How had she gotten so lucky to have friends like Kayla? To have a wonderful daughter, and now, to have a man she trusted and loved?

Even though Todd hadn't said the actual words to her yet, she understood well enough that he loved her. Or at least he cared deeply for her, enough that he wanted her and Simona in his life. Which meant more to her than if he had said those three words that neither Brock nor anyone else in her life had ever uttered to either her or Simona before.

CHAPTER 18

Over the next couple of weeks, he continued to work on turning his place into a home. Not just for himself, but for Olivia and, more importantly, Simona. Which meant his old schoolroom had to be updated and made safer. He couldn't believe some of the old things in there and how hazardous they were for kids of any age.

First, he found out that the paint on the walls was lead based. He'd hired a crew to come out and strip the walls so that he could put a fresh coat of safe paint on and hang up the old chalkboards. He'd thought about replacing them, but since the old ones were still in good condition, he figured they would do for now.

Olivia was true to her word. Not only did they have one night a week where it was just the two of them, but now, at least two to three nights a week, he got to hang out with both her and Simona.

It was becoming the standard that the two of them spent every Friday night at his place, which worked out perfectly, since Olivia's work schedule allowed them to spend all day Friday together.

On two occasions, they had gone out to East Haven Resort to go swimming and have picnics on the beach. He could tell that it was Simona's favorite place in the whole world because she often mentioned it two or three times when they were out there.

Since their talk, he'd noticed a huge change in Olivia. She was more open with him and seemed less afraid to tell him about her past. He felt more relaxed as well. He even opened up to her about how his life had changed after his father had passed. How his mother had twisted and grown colder and more distant.

They sat on his back patio, watching the sky change colors as the sun set over the town and talking about Olivia's fears about Simona going into second grade.

"Isn't second grade a lot like first?" he asked, unsure. He couldn't really remember anything before fifth grade.

Olivia rolled her eyes at him. "Seriously?" She smiled. "That's what Simona does if you ask her the same question."

"She's a diva all right." He smiled.

Olivia chuckled. "I wonder where she gets it?"

He reached over and wrapped his arm around her shoulders. He glanced through the sliding doors to where Simona was watching cartoons on the television and eating a yogurt. He could see she was totally engrossed in the show and smiled.

"She is pretty amazing," he said, turning back to Olivia.

"So are you. All the things you've seen and done in your life." She sighed. "I've never even been out of the States."

"You haven't?" He leaned in and kissed her. "We'll have to plan a trip. Where do you want to go?"

She tilted her head slightly as she thought about it for a moment.

"I've always wanted to go to Canada," she finally said.

He laughed. "Seriously? It's only a day's drive from here. Why haven't you gone?"

"Time, money, and, oh right. Can you imagine spending ten hours in a car with a six-year-old?" She smiled.

"Right." He nodded. "Okay, where in Canada?"

"Prince Edward Island." She rested her head back against his shoulder.

"*Anne of Green Gables* fan?" he asked.

She glanced up at him. "I can't wait until Simona is old enough to get hooked on the stories."

"When is her birthday?"

"July first."

He sat up a little. "That's only a week away."

"I know," Olivia answered.

"That doesn't give us a lot of time to plan the party."

Olivia frowned over at him. "Party?"

"Yes. Don't we need to order a cake, presents, invite people." He stood up and started pacing the deck as he ticked off everything that he believed they'd need for a seven-year-old's birthday celebration.

Olivia laughed and stood up to stop him from walking.

"Easy, I have everything handled." She rested her hands on his shoulders.

"You do?" He frowned, feeling a little let down that he hadn't been included in the details.

"Yes." She smiled. "Simona wants a swim party out at the resort. I worked everything out with Sarah months ago."

He relaxed slightly. "A pool party?" He could see the benefits of that. He could get her a gift... He stopped and turned to Olivia. "What sort of gift does she want? I mean, what do seven-year-old girls like, besides movies."

Olivia wrapped her arms around him. "We can go shopping together. I still have a few more things to get for the party."

"This weekend?" he asked, holding on to her.

"Sure." She rested her head back on his shoulder. "I love that you're so concerned about this." She looked up at him.

He brushed a strand of her dark hair away from her face and bent down to kiss her. "She means a lot to me. Both of you do."

Her entire body relaxed against his, and he knew that he'd won this small battle. Not too long ago she would have tensed.

"Let's go inside and finish watching the show with Simona," he suggested. The sun had fully set, leaving them in darkness.

Since it was the middle of the week, he knew his time with them that evening was limited. So he sat on his sofa, snuggling with the two girls in his life, and watched *Moana* for the third time that month.

Then he carried Simona out to Olivia's car and locked her in the car seat while she was dead asleep. He gave her a kiss on the forehead before kissing Olivia goodnight.

Since he was too revved up to head to bed, he worked on building the wood shelving for the pantry. When he was done hanging the last shelf, he was tired and sore. He had decided to paint them all white instead of staining them like he'd originally planned.

Tomorrow, he would conquer the bench with built-in cubbies under it for his mudroom. He'd ordered some rustic seahorse hooks for his coats and hats and wanted to stick with light blues and a nautical theme throughout the house. He'd found some whale's tail hooks as well but planned on putting those in the bathroom for towels. Olivia had actually picked them out for him along with a few sea-glass lamps and vases to go on the bookshelves.

The more he looked around the house, the more he realized it was beginning to feel like a home. Especially when Olivia and Simona were there.

For the next two days, he worked on the house while looking forward to that weekend and going gift shopping with Olivia. He'd done a little research online about what seven-year-old girls liked as gifts. There were so many choices, so many toys, games, or outfits to choose from. He was hoping Olivia would help him narrow down the choices by telling him what Simona liked or wanted.

Since Rowan had finished his remodel on the bathroom, he no longer ran into the man at the hardware store as much as he had before. But Todd was becoming familiar with a few other people in town.

He hadn't known who Eric Torre was at first, other than by name. He'd seen the guy walking around in his paint-covered jeans and shirts at the hardware store and had even thought about approaching him and asking him for a quote to paint the outside of his house since he'd seen the sign on the man's van for T&T Painting.

But then Dave, one of the workers at the hardware store, pointed Eric out. Since then, he'd noticed that the man was always staring him down, no doubt telling Brock every detail about him.

Thankfully, the man hadn't been any more trouble for Olivia. He had been sentenced to community service, and he'd seen the man on the side of the road in an orange vest, picking up trash along with a bunch of other people.

He didn't figure there was anything special about Eric, other than he knew everyone in town. Still, most people that knew him seemed to dismiss his behavior, as if the man had always acted crazy.

Even Olivia seemed to be over it. The only way Todd could be sure the man wasn't going to try anything else was to keep an eye on him. Which meant knowing everything about the man—where he lived, where he worked, and who his friends were.

He dug deep into the man's past. It wasn't hard, seeing as that is what Todd had spent most of the last ten years of his life doing for work. He and his team had been paid to know everything about their targets.

He even looked into Olivia's ex, Brock. After causing a fender bender while high, he'd led the police on a short chase and had ended up destroying two cruisers while he was at it. The chances of him getting out of prison this time were extremely slim.

The fact that he still blamed Olivia for his troubles weighed heavily on Todd. There was video of the man's court hearing where he punched a bailiff and yelled profanities, all while screaming that he'd get revenge on Olivia. Eric had been sitting in the audience, which assured Todd that Olivia's trouble with the duo wasn't over.

As far as his own troubles, there hadn't been any more word on the murders of his team members. He was still very watchful and continued to try and figure out who could be after them.

But the fact was, his team had gone on over thirty missions together. They had enemies everywhere, in more than a dozen countries.

Naturally, he made a list of the top possibilities. None, however, knew any of his team members' real names. Which meant either there was a leak or their covers had been blown during the mission. In his memory, he couldn't think of any mission that had gone sideways so badly. Except one.

Kimber. Shortly after he'd been exposed, another team had gone in and taken out her father, leaving no one to come after him or his team. Not even Kimber had known his real name.

There were other missions that had come close to going sideways but none where they had been as exposed.

All he could do was keep his eye out for anything out of the ordinary. In such a small town, that would normally be easy. But Silver Cove had been flooded the past few weeks with tourists, so he was sticking close to home. He was looking forward to going shopping this weekend with Olivia and for their standard Friday night sleepover.

With Simona's party next week, he'd figured that he would do something different this weekend with the girls. He wanted to take them out on a full day excursion but hadn't been sure what to do.

Then he'd run into Adam at the grocery store, and he'd started talking about taking his family out on Saturday on his sailboat. Adam convinced him to bring Olivia and Simona to tag along.

While he was standing in the bread aisle, he sent Olivia a text message and got her immediate reply that they were excited to go along. So he and Adam spent the rest of the time in the store planning out a full day's worth of food for four kids and four adults. He actually just stood back and let the man do what he was best at.

When he returned home, he had three loads full of groceries. It was satisfying to put everything away in his new pantry.

He'd made a point to purchase some of Simona's favorite snacks. He figured that a few days after Simona's birthday, he'd invite everyone over to his place to see all the work he'd done and to celebrate the Fourth of July at his place.

Adam mentioned that, normally, they'd get together on the boat, but since the group had grown so big, they hadn't planned anything yet. So he'd put the word out that the party was at his place. He had the perfect place for a large gathering of kids and parents. He figured he could grill out while the kids played games in the yard.

He would need some more tables and chairs for outside but there was still plenty of time to either purchase them or make a few picnic tables. He'd started rethinking his yard and doing yard work the following day.

He rebuilt part of the fence that had fallen over and had purchased some blooming flowers, including some lavender, to plant along the house. He'd been told at the nursery that lavender kept the bugs, including mosquitoes, away.

He spent an hour or so trimming bushes with his new hedge trimmer, making them all perfectly round. When he stood back and looked over the yard an hour before sunset, he realized how much better his yard and home looked than before.

He was standing in the middle of the road when a dark SUV pulled down the road and stopped in front of his garage.

"Evening," Javan said, smiling at him.

"Evening." He leaned on the side of the van. "I didn't know you were still around."

"Just got back. Boss wanted me to hang around for a while," Javan said.

"Oh?" Todd instantly grew worried.

"Nothing to worry about. He just has a hunch. My boss is never wrong, so I tend to listen to him," Javan added.

"Well, you're welcome to the room." He motioned to the garage. "If you need it."

"Thanks," Javan said with a nod. "You won't even know I'm here."

"Do you have a family?" he asked the man out of the blue.

"No, mon," Javan answered. "No woman has been able to tie me down."

Todd chuckled. "Sometimes it's nice to be tied down by a woman."

Javan slapped him on the shoulder, almost knocking Todd over completely, as he laughed.

"You doing some yard work? The place sure looks nice." Javan motioned to the house.

"Yeah, getting ready for a party here on the Fourth," Todd answered, looking over the yard once more. It did look good. He'd trimmed the yard down and had the sprinklers going now, and the entire area smelled of summer and fresh cut grass.

"Fourth?" Javan frowned. "Oh, right, Independence Day." Javan climbed out of the SUV. "I'll just make myself at home again. I'll park inside." He walked over and punched the code on the garage door.

"Let me know if there's anything I should be concerned about," Todd said.

"Will do." Javan waved and then climbed in the SUV and pulled it into the garage next to Todd's own car.

When Todd stepped inside the house, he realized he'd forgotten his cell phone inside. There were a few messages from Ethan telling him that he was sending Javan back down to stay with him for the next week as a precaution.

He replied that Javan had made it there. Then he read the message from Olivia and, instead of replying, called her.

"Evening," she answered on the second ring.

"Evening." He sat on the sofa and put his feet up. He hadn't realized how hard he'd worked, but now that he had stopped moving, his entire body ached. "Are you still at work?"

"Until ten. I only have a moment to talk." He heard the sound of the bell that chimed every time the store door was opened, signally customers had come in. "I wanted to tell you that Simona is staying with Crystal this weekend, so we're all set for our shopping trip."

"Wonderful," he said, knowing that she had to go.

"Talk to you later tonight," she said before hanging up.

An entire weekend together. Alone. He couldn't wait. With all of his house and yard work done already, he figured he could spend the entire weekend building up enough nerve to tell her just how he felt about her.

CHAPTER 19

Thursday nights at work were some of the busiest nights. Especially after dark. A steady stream of customers came and went, which normally made the time fly by. But tonight seemed slower than normal.

When she'd tried to call Todd, it had gone to his voice mail and she figured he was out in his yard mowing and hadn't heard it ring.

She was looking forward to spending an entire weekend with him, now that Crystal had agreed to take Simona out to the resort with her and Rory for the weekend.

It was so nice having people surrounding her that she trusted to care for her daughter. She may not have gotten the best deal with Brock but moving to Silver Cove had been the best decision of her life.

"Evening," she said to a pretty blonde woman who had strolled in. Instantly, she could tell the woman had a lot of money. Years of working retail had honed Olivia's skills at assessing people.

The cream-colored skirt and blouse were designer brand, as were the heeled cream sandals and matching bag. The outfit easily cost as much as Olivia's new car, maybe more if you accounted for the jewelry.

"Hello," the woman replied with a thick accent, one Olivia couldn't quite place.

"Is there something I can help you find tonight?" Olivia asked with a friendly tone.

"No, I am just looking," she answered, as if annoyed. There was a hint of Russian, but something else in her accent.

"If you find anything or have a question, let me know." Olivia moved behind the counter. She knew that some customers liked their space, and she figured this woman was one of them.

The woman walked up and down each aisle, as if bored or shocked with everything in the store. Why had she even come in? It wasn't as if the outside of Serenity's Attic didn't make it obvious what was on the inside. The store was painted bright colors, a clear sign of what it held inside.

Olivia was about to ask her if she was looking for anything in particular, but more customers came in and she turned her attention towards them instead. The woman disappeared from the store while she was busy.

The couple that had come in purchased several bottles of oils and lotions and booked a couple's massage for the following evening.

Later, when she walked up to the house, Simona fast asleep on her hip, she was so tired and half asleep that she almost didn't notice that her back door was standing wide open.

Her entire body shook and for a moment, she froze, unsure of what to do. Then her daughter shifted ever so slightly, and she took off running and didn't stop until she was standing in front of Crystal's place, breathless, with Simona crying her name.

"What is it? What's happened?" Crystal asked when she opened the door to them.

"There… my door… someone…" Olivia managed to say.

"Rory." Crystal turned to her husband.

"On it," he said, pulling out his phone.

"Come on inside." Crystal took Simona from her arms, almost having to pry her free from her death grip.

"It's Brock," she gasped, "he's come to take her…"

"Shhh, now," Crystal said, hugging the now quieted Simona close. "There's no use in speculating."

"The police are on their way, so is Todd," Rory said calmly. "I figured he'd want to know."

"Thanks," she said when Rory handed her a glass of water.

"I'm just going to go take Simona up to bed," Crystal said calmly. "You've got this?" she asked Rory, who nodded. He sat next to Olivia and wrapped his arms around her.

"Did you run all the way here?" he asked her.

"I…" She blinked a few times.

"That's, like, two miles." Rory smiled. "Remind me to have you fill in for me the next time Crystal makes me sign up for a 5K."

She relaxed slightly and then smiled knowing that Rory was purposely trying to make her feel at ease.

"My back door was open," she said, looking down into the glass of water. "Someone was in the house."

"Do you know that for sure? Did you see someone?"

"No." She glanced up at the man and, as she had a few times before, compared him to her own father. Rory Sinclair was anything but old looking. He was the type of man you see on the cover of those gentlemen magazines. Demure. Poised. Sexy as hell. He had several silver streaks running through his brown hair, the only sign of his middle age.

"What do you say to having something a little stronger?"

He stood up suddenly and walked over to the small built-in bar area. "Scotch?"

"A shot of tequila," she answered, knowing she would need the liquid courage if she was going to return home that night.

By the time she downed the shot, the police were there, knocking on the door. Moments later, Todd rushed in.

"Olivia?" he called out from the doorway.

"In here." She stood up and welcomed his embrace. She started shivering when his arms wrapped around her. "What happened?" he asked into her hair.

"Someone broke into my house."

"Well, now," Scott started, "we don't know that for sure. Tom's over there now checking the place out."

"My back door was wide open," she said, as Todd moved over and sat with her on the sofa.

"Where's Simona?" he asked.

"Fast asleep upstairs," Crystal said as she walked back into the room. "She's safe. I told her you got scared, that's all, and that she was going to spend the night here, with us."

"Thank you." Olivia relaxed back into Todd's embrace. "I... didn't know where else to go. You were the closest."

"She ran," Rory offered.

"My keys were in my hand, but... I froze up. Didn't even think about driving." She closed her eyes, feeling stupid. All she'd been thinking about was keeping Simona away from Brock.

"It's not Brock," Todd said softly. "He's in jail in Boston."

She glanced over at him. "How do you know that?"

"I... I'm keeping tabs on him," Todd said, looking slightly embarrassed. "I just needed to know that he wasn't going to come after you or Simona."

Olivia's heart jumped in her chest as she reached for him and pulled him into a hug again. "Thank you," she said softly.

"Are you okay?" he asked.

"Yes, I think I spooked myself over nothing." She closed her eyes. "I probably left the door unlocked and it blew open."

The more she thought about it, the more she convinced herself that that was the case.

"Why don't you start at the beginning," Scott suggested, "while we wait for Tom to get here."

When Tom arrived, less than half an hour later, she ran through everything that had happened.

"Well, I couldn't find anything out of place, but it was pretty obvious that someone broke in," Tom informed them when he arrived.

"How?" both she and Todd asked at the same time.

"Your door lock is in pieces. Someone shattered it." He shook his head. "It's the damnedest thing. The entire door handle is shattered, like it was made out of glass."

She felt Todd stiffen next to her.

"But nothing was taken? The television? My laptop was on the kitchen counter," she asked.

"It's all there." Tom sighed. "But in the next few days, if you happen to find something missing, let us know."

"Thanks." Todd stood up and shook Tom's hand.

"I shut the door and secured your deadbolt with the spare key you told me about." He held out the keyring she kept hidden in an old tree stump by her back door. She knew better than to keep a hide-a-key under the mat or a fake rock, but the tree stump was so out of the ordinary, she figured no one would think to look there. Apparently, she'd been correct, since whoever had broken in hadn't known about it.

"Why don't you and Simona come stay with me for the rest of the night?" Todd suggested.

She wanted desperately to say yes, but something had her shaking her head no, instead.

"If I don't go back now, I'll become too afraid to be there by myself after dark. This is my home. I won't let someone run me out of it because of fear," she said confidently.

"I'll go with you," Todd agreed. "Don't argue," he added when she opened her mouth.

She shook her head again. "No, I won't argue. I'd appreciate it."

"Simona can stay here for the night. I'd hate to wake her up again," Crystal added. "Besides, I promised her cinnamon rolls for breakfast."

"You did?" Rory jumped in eagerly, then he cleared his throat and tried to act like he wasn't excited himself.

Crystal smiled. "You can have one."

Rory nodded. "I'll take it."

"We'll stop by later tomorrow to get her things if she needs them. Take your time shopping tomorrow. She'll be here when you get back." Crystal winked at them. "I'm going to spoil Simona all day long."

"Thank you." Olivia jumped up and hugged both Crystal and Rory. "I don't know what I would do if you two weren't here for us."

"Go on." Crystal waved her away after the hug. "Take back your home and get some sleep."

She followed Todd outside, her hand resting comfortably in his.

"Did you really run all the way here holding Simona?" he asked as he opened his car door for her.

"Yes," she sighed. "My back will be paying for it tomorrow."

He climbed in behind the wheel and then turned to her. "I'm glad the two of you are safe."

She nodded, feeling tired and emotional all at once. "Do you think it was Eric?"

He frowned and was quiet for a moment while he drove back to her place.

"It could be," he finally said.

"But… something in your voice tells me you don't think it was. What is it?" she asked, glancing over at him.

"I'm not sure. I'd like to wait and see once we get there. There's just something about the way Tom described the lock being broken that… sits strangely with me," Todd admitted.

"Okay." She rested her head back and tried not to think about someone else walking through her home. Combing through her things. Maybe even stealing something private.

Todd parked beside her car and helped her climb out. Just thinking about someone being in her house had her shivering against the warm night air.

"Cold?" he asked her, wrapping his arms around her.

"Just… tired," she said. Todd took her keys from her and opened the back door, then he flipped on the kitchen light. While she stood just outside, he examined the lock.

"Want me to go through the house once more?" he asked her.

"No." She took a deep breath and then stepped inside. A wave of joy and fear mixed deep in her gut.

Joy because this was her place. Hers alone. She'd done this. She'd paid for every single item in it. She'd painted every wall, hung every picture. No one could ever take that from her. Fear because she knew just how close she'd come to losing it. If Brock or Eric thought that they could intimidate her, well, they were right. All it took was the fear of Simona's safety, and she'd gladly have kept running and left it all behind.

Nothing mattered more to her than her daughter.

Strong arms wrapped around her from behind, causing her to jump slightly.

"You okay?" Todd asked, resting his chin on her shoulder.

"Hm." She nodded as tears rolled down her face slowly. "I'd gladly give it all up, just to know that she was safe."

He turned her towards him and then gently used his thumb to wipe the tears away.

"You won't have to." He kissed her wet cheeks. "I'm here. You have people that love you and would do anything and everything to see that you and Simona are safe."

She nodded, closing her eyes tight to hold in the love she felt from her friends. From him.

If she could bottle it up, she would, that feeling of knowing someone else was looking out for you and yours. How long had she searched in life for just that?

Todd nudged her back and looked down into her face. "Is it okay if I stay here tonight?"

"Yes." She chuckled. "There is no way I'm going to be able to sleep without you here."

His smile was instant. "Then we don't have to sleep." His hands started roaming over her, and she felt her entire body melt against his.

"Todd," she moaned when he dipped his hand under her pants.

"You're already wet for me," he said against her ear just before his mouth ran over her skin. "I want to feel you come for me. Just like this." He nudged her pants down her legs. "Right here." He backed her up to the kitchen counter. "I want to taste you on my tongue, to smell your sweet pussy and feel you wrap your legs around my shoulders."

While he talked, she could imagine everything he told her he wanted from her, everything he wanted to do to her.

He nudged her pants all the way off her, taking a moment

to remove her shoes and kissing a trail up her legs, and she closed her eyes and enjoyed the feeling of being cherished.

Then he was slipping his fingers and tongue into her, and she cried out his name as she convulsed just like he'd demanded.

She felt light-headed and relaxed in his hold as he carried her into her bedroom. She was thankful that she'd taken a moment earlier that morning to make her bed and clean up a little.

"I can't believe how lucky I am to be here with you, like this," he said, looking down at her.

"Todd." His name was half moan and half plea. "I need…"

"I know," he said, setting her down on the edge of the bed and then standing back to remove his shirt, shoes, and jeans.

Her entire body started vibrating again at just seeing him like that. He was lean, toned, and full of muscles she liked to play with.

Reaching up, she ran her fingertips over him, slowly enjoying the way he responded to her touch.

Taking his hand in hers, she pulled him down onto the bed until he covered her.

"This means something," he said, looking down into her eyes.

"Yes," she agreed.

"Olivia." He stopped when she tried to pull him into her. "I've never felt this way before."

She smiled up at him, then slipped her fingers into his hair and nudged him closer until they were a breath away.

"I know. I love you too," she said softly, just before he plunged into her.

CHAPTER 20

Having the entire day with the woman he loved was perfect. It was by far one of the best days in his life.

They weren't due to pick up Simona at Crystal's until around five, and he was looking forward to spending the following day on the boat with both of his ladies.

Riding with Olivia into the city once more, they talked about how likely it was that Eric had broken into her place and hadn't touched a thing.

Since they were in town, they stopped off and purchased new locks for all of her doors, as well as a doorbell camera kit.

When they walked into the kids' store, he was a little overwhelmed until Olivia told him that half of the store was the boy's section and half was for girls. Then it was broken down by age groups. Which meant, there was only five aisles for them to wander through to pick something out for Simona.

He was looking at toys and dolls of all her favorite characters when he spotted the camera. It was a version of the old Polaroids but made for kids, and it was the color of Elsa's dress.

He remembered how much Simona had enjoyed using his phone to take pictures previous weekend when he'd been working in the yard. The camera was a perfect gift.

"That's perfect," Olivia said when he showed it to her.

"I purchased a few packs of film for her too." He showed her the handful of extra film he'd grabbed.

Olivia laughed. "A few? You have a dozen."

He shrugged. "I don't want you to have to come back here anytime soon."

"I can probably order them online," she suggested.

"True, but this way you don't have to for a while."

"She's going to love it." Olivia smiled as she set a box of cookie cutters in the shape of her favorite characters in the cart. "I was going to make sugar cookies and have all of her friends decorate them during the party."

"Great idea. I guess I never asked you how many kids were actually coming to the party."

Olivia took a deep breath. "Twenty. So far."

"Twenty?" he exclaimed. How are we going to keep track of them all?"

She laughed. "Luckily, their parents are all going to be there too. Sarah has arranged access for the adults, so we won't be bombarded with other people's kids."

"Not that I couldn't handle a few. I mean, watching Kayla and Rowan's kids with Simona was nice." He pulled her close to him in the middle of the aisle. "Made me realize that three kids, two girls and one boy, is the perfect dynamics for a family," he said easily.

She was quiet for a while. "You... want three kids?"

"Sure," he said as he started walking down the toy aisle again. "Don't you want more?"

She caught up with him, and he could tell she was unsure

of what to say. "I… suppose. I mean, sure." She shrugged casually.

He turned down the boy aisle and smiled at all the trucks and building blocks. "You know, girls like playing with these things too."

"Sure, they do. I don't really think the stores have caught on though," Olivia joked.

"They make pink guns and power tools; you'd think they could easily make pink GI Joes," he suggested.

"They do. It's called GI Jane." She motioned to the action figures.

"Yeah, but… It's not the same." He leaned closer to her. "Unless you buy both. Then…" He wiggled his eyebrows, and she laughed.

They stopped in town for burgers for lunch and then went back to her place. She wrapped up the gifts while he replaced her front door handle and installed her new door-bell camera system.

"You know, you two could come stay at my place tonight?" he offered when she was about to leave to go pick up Simona from Crystal's place.

"Thank you, but I think we're okay." She wrapped her arms around his waist. "We wouldn't say no to you staying here though."

"I'll head home and grab everything we need for our trip tomorrow." He smiled. "I'm really looking forward to sailing again. It's been years since I've been out on the water."

"Adam's boat is amazing. Not to mention there is always some amazing food to go along with it. He usually catches lunch, then grills it up right there," Olivia said. "Oh, and grand-mère Sonya will be there. I hear she's been looking forward to seeing how your French has progressed."

He chuckled and in fluent French, said. "I'll have to impress her with it then."

Olivia shrugged. "You have me beat."

"Since there will be four kids, we decided on turkey sandwiches. But Adam was going to make a couple sides to go with it all. There was mention of salad noodles of some kind." He tried to remember what Adam had called it.

"Asian noodle salad?" Olivia smiled. "Yum."

"I'll trust you." He smiled. "Go get our girl. I'll go home and grab what we need." Bending, he kissed her. "Be back soon."

Floating on a high, he drove back to his place. He loved this time of night, coming home to the house when the sun was setting behind the garage, which bathed his home in bright colors.

Someday soon, he was going to ask Olivia and Simona to move in with him. He wanted more than anything for this to be their home. To have those two extra kids he'd talked to her about. Their kids. All three of them, since he already thought of Simona as his.

He stepped in the back door, removed his shoes, and put them in the cubbies below the bench that he'd built in the mudroom. He was so proud of the work that he'd done around the place. It was finally starting to feel like home. Maybe it was because Olivia and Simona were spending more and more time there.

He was so preoccupied with dreaming about his perfect life with Olivia and Simona that he didn't register something was wrong until he felt the sharp pain in his side. Instantly, his heart began to race as the electric current charged through his entire body, forcing all his limbs to freeze up until, finally, he felt himself fading into blackness.

When he woke, he was groggy and unsure of what had happened. That changed quickly when he tried to move and realized that his hands were tied down. His entire body jumped to alert.

Looking around, he realized he was no longer in his home. Even though it was dark, he knew that he had to be on a boat somewhere, since the entire room was slowly swaying with the movement of the ocean. Either that or the taser he'd been shocked with had extra high voltage and had done some damage to his brain.

If this was a boat, it had to be a fairly large one since the room was easily as big as his bedroom. He listened for any sounds other than water lapping outside but didn't hear anything. No boat motors, which meant he'd been out for a time. Long enough for whoever had taken him to drag him out of the house and onto a boat. Had they docked the boat behind his place? Or loaded him in a van and then hauled him into a boat at the town's docks? If it were the latter, he could still be at the docks.

He tried wiggling his way out of his restraints, which by the feel of them were thick wiry ropes tied very tightly around not only his wrists and arms, but his thighs, calves, and ankles. He realized he was still shoeless.

He continued to fight against his restraints, letting the ropes cut into his skin in a desperate attempt to break free.

Hearing a noise, he looked up and saw a dark figure step into the room from the door directly in front of him. He could see a flash of dim light coming from the other room or from outside.

He waited a heartbeat, then a light flashed on in the room and he knew he was screwed. Standing across from him in a flowing red jumpsuit stood Kimber Ivanov, daughter of Maxim Ivanov, oligarch of the Chukotka Province in Russia. Well, ex-oligarch, at any rate, since the man had been killed by his team shortly after he'd escaped the family's clutches.

"Kimber." He smiled, knowing that his situation couldn't get any worse. Scratch that, he thought quickly. Kimber could have gone after Olivia or Simona. His mind jumped back to the door handle he'd replaced at Olivia's place and knew that he should have guessed that it was Kimber who had broken in. After all, that was how he'd broken into her place years ago.

"Adrian." She narrowed her eyes. "Or should I say, Todd O'Brien." She said his name as if it tasted bad in her mouth. She leaned on a table and looked down at her perfectly manicured fingernails, the same color red as her outfit. "Don't you think it's about time we had a little chat?"

"If I remember correctly, last time we chatted… you tried to kill me," he said smoothly. There was always a way out. There had to be a way out this time. His future with Olivia and Simona depended on it. He just had to think.

"You were spying on my father." She shifted slightly. Her thick Russian accent didn't hinder his understanding of her words. After all, he'd spent more than six months living with her. Sleeping with her. Watching every move that she and her family made. "I don't suppose you had anything to do with his death, two weeks after you disappeared?"

"Your father's dead?" he asked, trying to sound surprised.

Her eyes narrowed ever so slightly, and he understood that she didn't believe him.

"No," he replied, meaning it. "I was still in the hospital when I got word of his death."

Her eyes relaxed and she nodded. "Yes, I know this to be true."

"Why come after me?" He glanced down at the ropes. "Can't we be civil?" He smiled. "Like old times?" He tried for charm.

Her eyes narrowed again. "You are with this other woman now, no?" she asked, watching him closely.

He froze. His heart jumped in his chest, no doubt beating loud enough that she could hear it clearly across the room. Now that the room was fully lit, he could see it was a suite on a yacht. He had no doubt that more money had been spent decorating this one space than he'd spent redoing his entire house.

Maxim Ivanov, when he'd been alive, had ruled over the province with fear and with death. Most of his subjects were spied on, imprisoned, poisoned, or had their wealth turned over to the state if they questioned anything. Especially Ivanov himself.

While he and his daughter enjoyed the wealth and titles of the land, his subjects suffered greatly. When the US government had gotten reports that Ivanov was planning a blockade of the Bering Strait, which included seizing all boats in the area and all of Alaska's harbors, his team was sent it to confirm the rumors.

The night that he'd finally confirmed those reports had been the night Kimber had found out what he was. He'd believed that she loved him, that she would overlook his deceit. Instead, she'd turned him in to her father and helped as he'd been beaten and hauled away for death.

Then he thought of Olivia and realized that there was no doubt in his mind just how she felt about him. He knew fully that she loved him as much as he loved her. He hoped that she'd understand what had happened to him. Why he'd have to break his promise to her about breaking her heart.

"Yes," he finally answered Kimber, "I'm with Olivia."

"She is plain. Boring." Kimber shifted slightly. "Her life is… chaotic. She has a daughter, no? Where is her man?"

"He's… in jail," he said, knowing there was nothing he could do now to protect them. She'd walked through their house already. Kimber probably had gotten all the information she'd needed on Olivia and Simona last night.

"Why are you here?" he asked finally.

Kimber glanced down at her fingernails again. "I would

think that was obvious," she said, as if bored. "You have something I want."

"Which is?" he asked, feeling his stomach turn.

She stood up straight and moved slowly towards him, her hips swaying with each step that she took. When she leaned in close to his face, he smelled her favorite expensive perfume. The kind she'd always worn when they'd been together. Instead of being turned on, he felt his stomach revolt and had to swallow down the bile that rose.

Her red lips hovered just above his as she pinched his face in her fingers, holding him still.

"You're life." She smiled. "But I think first"—her dark eyes ran over his face—"I'll have some fun." She leaned in and covered his mouth with hers.

Moments seemed to pass by as he held still, willing her to make one mistake to allow him to break free, to rush back to Olivia and the life he wanted.

Then the door burst open, and he watched in horror as Olivia was shoved into the room by a large man. Kimber didn't release him or the kiss. Instead, she held his face tightly in her fingers as she deepened the kiss, darting her tongue over his lips and breaking through to explore the inside of his mouth.

He jerked several times, trying to cry out to Olivia, to get her to run, to hide, to escape. But Kimber kept him hostage. Locked in a one-way kiss.

When Kimber finally leaned back, freeing him, she smiled and turned to look down at Olivia, who was sitting on the floor, staring daggers into Kimber's back.

"Oh good, you made it," Kimber said, as if Olivia had just shown up late for a party. "I do hope Nicholai wasn't too rough with you."

"Where's Simona?" Todd cried out, only to have Kimber jerk around and backhand him. Her fingers were always covered in large, jeweled rings, and he felt them tear his skin open.

"She's safe," Olivia said as she stood up. "I suppose you're Kimber?" she said clearly.

He watched in amazement as the woman he loved squared off with the largest deadliest spider he'd ever fallen for.

"Kimber Ivanov," Kimber answered proudly.

"Is that name supposed to mean anything?" Olivia said with a slight smile, then tilted her head. "You came into my store the other day. Did you break into my home too?"

Kimber chuckled. "You have such a small life." Kimber sighed and shook her head. "I don't know why Adrian, oh"—Kimber smiled again—"I mean Todd would waste his time with you. I suppose he was bored."

He watched Olivia's reaction and was pleased when she didn't fall for Kimber's trap.

"I'm guessing you're just another job from Todd's past. Someone he was paid to infiltrate to gain secrets." Olivia smiled. "Is that what this is about?" She motioned around her. "You can't take no for an answer?"

Kimber jerked towards Olivia, but Olivia easily side-stepped and twisted away from her advance. Unfortunately, Nicholai hadn't left the room and grabbed Olivia's arms to hold her still.

"It's such a shame that you have to have a man do your dirty work for you." Olivia laughed as Nicholai jerked her arms behind her.

"Olivia," Todd warned only to have her shoot a look at him that told him to stay out of it. He didn't know what she was doing, but whatever it was, he wasn't going to get in the way. He'd seen her give that same look to Simona several times and knew the consequences of the mom look.

"I don't need a man to do anything for me." Kimber waved Nicholai off.

"Right," Olivia said sarcastically. "I suppose Nicholai was the one that killed Todd's team members. After all"—Olivia ran her eyes over Kimber's attire—"a woman of your… fragile standing couldn't kidnap and kill three members of an elite team, let alone a single urban mother."

Kimber laughed. "Oh, I didn't need any man to help out. It was easy, with this." Kimber pulled out a long taser stick from her jumpsuit pocket. "I had this made just for me." She turned it on and Olivia jumped back slightly.

"So, you what? Tased them, dragged them into the van, and murdered them? All for what? To get back at Todd?" Olivia asked. "Are they the ones who told you how to find Todd?"

"The first two didn't break." Kimber made a tsking noise. "But the third…" She smiled, then glanced back at Todd as her smile fell away. "He owes me," Kimber hissed. It was the first sign that she was losing her temper. He'd only witnessed it one other time before, the night she'd used her high heels to kick and stab him unconscious as he lay tied up on the ground.

"Oh, I see." Olivia smiled and glanced at him. Suddenly, he could see clearly what she was doing. Olivia was stalling. Whatever she had planned, he knew she needed help. "You knocked them out and then Nicholai dragged them around? I bet you haven't killed anyone."

"You know, I think you are toying with me." Kimber moved closer to Olivia, the taser held between them.

Whatever she was going to do, he either had to help her or come up with his own plan. All that mattered to him now was getting Olivia out of here safe. Even if it meant sacrificing himself.

CHAPTER 21

Shit. Olivia was struggling to keep away from that taser and away from the gorilla of a man, Nicholai. It was his beefy arms that had grabbed her from Todd's house. Even though she'd walked willingly into the trap, she'd been shocked at how large the man was, easily as big as Ethan had been.

When Javan had shown up at Crystal's house while she'd been there to grab Simona, she'd instantly been worried. Javan had a busted nose and a bloody lip and had obviously been in a fight.

He'd explained how he'd been attacked and tied up in the apartment above Todd's garage, and had to watch on the monitors as Todd had been kidnapped.

Olivia had panicked. Full on lost-her-shit kind of panic. Like last night when she'd taken off with Simona in her arms. She wanted to rush into action. Rush to Todd's place to look for him.

Instead, she'd been convinced to wait for Ethan to arrive. The man had been on his way there after following a lead in Texas.

So, she'd waited, holding Simona as tightly as she could for almost an hour before Ethan finally walked through the door at Crystal's place. By that time, all her friends had gathered, after hearing the news about Todd's kidnapping.

They were surrounded by friends and people she deemed family.

There had been speculation as to who had taken him, but until Ethan walked in with a picture and proof, none had even come close to the truth.

When Ethan had mentioned the name Kimber Ivanov, her first thought had been of the pretty blonde Russian that had come into her store the other day. Then Ethan had shown her a picture, and she'd confirmed that it was the same woman.

"There's been a yacht floating off the edge of the island for a few days," Sarah had jumped in. "My staff claims that some Russians were trying to dock the large vessel at our pier the other night."

"That would go along with my intel," Ethan had agreed. "It appears that they rented a van and drove to San Diego and then back to Texas, but then, the trail dried up."

"Do you think they sailed here from Texas?" Olivia asked.

"It would only take a little over a week," Ethan supplied.

"What do we do to get him back?" she asked, tears stinging her eyes. "I need him back."

"Mommy, is Todd okay?" Simona asked.

"I don't know, baby." She hugged her daughter again. "I'm going to do everything I can to get him back."

Simona started to cry. "I don't want anything for my birthday, except for Todd."

"Oh, baby." She closed her eyes and held onto her daughter. "We'll get him back."

"There is a chance," Ethan said. "It's slim and might be dangerous."

"I'll do it." Olivia jumped up. "If there's a chance we'll get him back."

"No," Crystal and Sarah said at the same time. "Let us…"

"This is for me," Olivia said. "He belongs to us." She looked at her daughter, then turned to Ethan. "What do I need to do?"

He'd taken a deep breath and then answered. "Get kidnapped."

So, here she was. Stalling for time. Waiting for the unseen boats outside to surround the massive yacht that she'd been dragged to.

The only way she knew how to stall was a classic catfight. Oh, she'd seen enough Bond movies to understand that the villainess would use her and the hero's past to try and damage true love. And at this point, she was pretty damn sure that's what was between her and Todd.

She'd witnessed the grotesque display with that kiss when she'd been shoved into the room.

Todd had looked disgusted during the kiss, then he'd seen her, and his look had changed to full blown worry.

Now she was having a hell of a time distracting Kimber. Especially after she pulled out the taser. If Olivia got tasered, there was no way they would hear the woman's confession on the wire that she was wearing in her hair.

Nicholai had searched her, just as Ethan had explained he would. She'd closed her eyes and held her breath while his beefy hands ran over her breasts, her buttocks, thankfully, not once had he run his fingers through her dark locks to expose the hairpiece that hid the device.

"I'm not as fragile as you think." Kimber finally took the bait and tossed the taser aside.

Olivia watched as the woman stepped out of her red high heels and started moving towards her.

"Oh, right." Olivia shook her head. "This is a fair fight. With Nicholai here."

Kimber barked something in Russian at the man, which had him moving back away from Olivia and standing on the other side of the room.

Turning back to Kimber, Olivia allowed her body to remember all of the moves she'd learned in the self-defense class she and Crystal had taken shortly after Brock had been arrested and her arm had healed.

She took the first blow to her chin and almost landed on her butt. The second blow was more of a slap and bounced off Olivia's shoulder.

Kimber used her long nails to scratch Olivia's arm, causing blood to squirt out and land directly on the woman's face.

"I draw first blood," Kimber said with a smile. "You are weak, just like Adrian."

Olivia used the moment the woman was distracted while she spoke to twist and kick out, knocking her onto her ass. Then she kicked out with her foot and hit the woman's chin, knocking her head backwards.

When Kimber recovered, Olivia smiled at the empty space where one of her perfectly white teeth used to be. Blood spurted from the gaping hole.

"You bitch." Kimber wiped her mouth and jumped up to rush towards the taser.

"Am I too much for you to handle now?" Olivia teased, fear spiking as Kimber grew inches from getting the taser.

She relaxed when Kimber turned back around and started moving towards her instead.

"When this is all over, I am going to enjoy watching the fish eat your corpse. Then I'll dangle your daughter over the edge of the boat as the sharks circle and slowly bite her to pieces," Kimber said while blood flowed from the spot where her front tooth used to be.

"You will never touch my daughter," Olivia said, sidestepping another blow, then using her elbow to knock Kimber onto her ass again. She knew better than to get too close to the woman. She didn't want to be pulled down onto the ground.

Olivia's best moves involved twisting away and kicking. Or so her self-defense coach had informed her. She allowed Kimber to stand up and square off once more.

"You are nothing!" Kimber screamed as she threw herself at Olivia.

Olivia fell backwards, bouncing off the wall while taking the scrapes and slaps Kimber used on her.

She was too close to fight back the way she knew. So instead, she did what she could. She kicked, pulled hair, and even bit her way free. She pushed Kimber to the ground and used her own weight to pin the woman down.

When Kimber yelled something in Russian, Olivia knew she was in trouble and glanced up to brace herself for Nicholai's attack. Instead, she watched in horror as Todd yelled. "Leave her alone!" and threw himself, chair and all, at Nicholai.

Both men flew across the room and landed in a tangled heap on the floor. The chair that had been holding Todd down shattered into pieces.

Nicholai tried to get up, but now that Todd was free, he sat on the man and started throwing powerful blows at the man's head.

Olivia's hair was yanked back as Kimber jerked out from under her. She'd been so distracted watching and worrying about Todd that she'd forgotten she was sitting on Kimber.

For the next few moments, Olivia did everything she

could, used every move she had in her arsenal, to overcome Kimber.

She'd finally gotten the woman under her again when the door to the room flew open.

"Get on the ground now!" multiple masked men in all black yelled into the room.

Olivia jerked her hands into the air and did as she was asked. Only to have Kimber throw one last sucker punch, slamming her head back against the wall until she saw stars.

"Olivia?" Todd's face appeared directly in front of hers. His lip was bloody, and his eye was swollen. "Honey, look at me."

"Todd? Did we win?" she asked, holding onto her head.

"Yeah, baby. We won." He smiled at her.

"You're bleeding." She lifted her hand and touched his lip.

"No, it's lipstick," he assured her as he wiped his mouth clean. "I might have a black eye though."

She smiled. "Me too." She touched her left eye and he laughed. "You fight like a champ."

"Not like a girl?" she asked, as every part of her body began to ache.

"Hell no." He leaned in and brushed his lips across her forehead. "Remind me to never cross you."

She smiled and looked around. "Where'd Kimber and Nicholai go?"

"They've been taken away. Ethan's team took them outside." He wrapped his arms around her again. "What were you thinking?" He leaned back. "Putting yourself in danger like that."

"I was thinking of you." She stood up with his help and started to dust off her jeans, only to realize they were beyond ruined. So were her shirt and shoes. Everything she wore was ripped or covered in blood.

"You have to think of Simona." He took her shoulders lightly and turned her towards him. "She needs a mother."

Olivia's eyes narrowed. "She needs a father too, and I had hoped that you would fill that position."

Todd remained silent for a moment. "You…" He swallowed. "You want me to be Simona's father?"

"Yes," she said rolling her eyes. "I really had hoped you weren't this dense," she added with a smile.

"You put yourself in danger to save me." He pulled her into his arms.

"Don't make me regret it." She kissed him.

"I was going to ask you to marry me on the Fourth," he said as he rested his forehead against hers. "I figured that way, if you said no, I could use the excuse of not hearing you over the fireworks I had planned to set off."

She smiled. "What if I said yes now, so you know my answer ahead of time?"

He grinned. "Does that mean I still have to get down on my knee to ask?"

"Yes," she said. She kissed him again. "And this time, I want a big fancy wedding. White dress, bridesmaids, and all."

"That can be arranged. I know your family wouldn't want it any other way."

"Oh!" she gasped. "My family." She tried to jerk out of his arms. "They're probably worried sick. We have to…"

He took her hand and followed her outside.

"There's a boat ready to take you back to the harbor." Ethan came out of the dark and motioned to a small dinghy attached to the yacht.

She pulled off the hairpiece that was, at this point, hanging from her head and handed it to Ethan. Then she climbed down the ladder and sat next to Todd on the small boat.

They held onto one another as they rode back to Silver

Creek docks. When they grew closer, she noticed that everyone they knew stood under the lights, waiting for them.

Crystal was holding onto Rory, who held Simona in his arms. Sarah and Ben, Lilly and Adam, and Kayla and Rowan waited with all of their kids gathered around them.

When they saw them coming, they all broke out in cheers as Olivia and Todd started waving.

"Mommy!" Simona jumped into her arms when she stepped onto the dock, causing Olivia to hiss with pain. Todd snagged Simona from her grasp and spun her around to distract her from Olivia's pain. When he stopped spinning her, he wrapped an arm around Olivia's shoulders.

"Your mommy has agreed to let me be your daddy," he told Simona.

Her daughter looked up at her with big eyes. "You have?"

"Yes," Olivia answered with a smile. "If it's okay with you?"

"Yes!" Simona started bouncing in Todd's arms. "It's the best birthday present ever!" Simona shouted.

"This calls for a celebration. What do you say to an early birthday cake at our house?" Crystal suggested. "Your mommy and your new daddy can shower and change into some clean clothes while we dish up some ice cream?"

"Yes!" all the kids shouted as they started dancing around.

Half an hour later, Olivia stood under the hot water in Crystal's guest room shower, letting it wash over her sore muscles and bruised body.

Warm hands gripped her waist and pulled her body back into a hard, powerful chest.

"Feel better?" Todd asked.

"Not really." She laughed. "Every single part of me hurts. My only prize is knowing that I still have all of my teeth and"—he turned in his hold and wrapped her arms around him—"you." She kissed him as he chuckled.

"Marry me," he said softly against her lips.

"I've already said yes," she reminded him.

He smiled. "I know, but I was afraid I was concussed and imagined it all." He kissed her again.

"In that case, you can ask me as many times as you want. The answer will always be yes." She leaned up on her toes and brushed her lips softly against his.

"How is it that every part of me hurts?" he asked.

She laughed and then hissed when her ribs ached. "I think you need to look at getting that hot tub we talked about installed this weekend."

"Done."

"We'd better go downstairs. I hear that after the kids are shuffled up to bed, the adults are going to have a story time where we get to fill them in on every detail of what happened on the yacht."

"Oh fun. I get to tell them how you kicked Russian butt." He sighed. "The kids are going to love having a sleepover."

She smiled. "Crystal sure knows how to throw a party."

They got out of the shower, dressed in the borrowed clothes, and made their way downstairs, where all of the kids were enjoying cake and ice cream and a movie.

A plate with a large piece of chocolate cake was thrust into her hands along with a large scoop of vanilla ice cream.

"Coffee?" Kayla asked.

"If I'm going to relive what happened on the boat, yes." She sat down at the table and dug into the treat.

"Mommy, CJ says you killed a Russian spy," Simona said, rushing over her.

Olivia laughed. "I didn't kill anyone. But I did knock her tooth out."

Simona's eyes grew big. "You did? Was it her grown-up tooth?"

Olivia laughed and pulled her daughter into her lap. "Yes, it was."

Todd's hand reached out and took hers. "Your mother is a hero. She saved my life."

"She did?" Simona asked.

"Yes," Todd said, winking at Olivia. "She did."

Breaking Travis

Roping Ryan

Wild Bride

Corey's Catch

Tessa's Turn

Saving Trace

The Grayton Series

Last Resort

Someday Beach

Rip Current

In Too Deep

Swept Away

High Tide

Lucky Series

Unlucky In Love

Sweet Resolve

Best of Luck

A Little Luck

Christmas Wish

Silver Cove Series

Silver Lining

French Kiss

Happy Accident

Hidden Charm

A Silver Cove Christmas

Sweet Surrender

Second Chances

Entangled Series – Paranormal Romance

The Awakening

The Beckoning

The Ascension

The Presence

The Calling

The Chosen

Haven, Montana Series

Closer to You

Never Let Go

Holding On

Coming Home

The Hard Way

Pride Oregon Series

A Dash of Love

My Kind of Love

Season of Love

Tis the Season

Dare to Love

Where I Belong

Because of Love

A Thing Called Love

First Comes Love

Someone to Love

Wildflowers Series

Summer Nights

Summer Heat

Summer Secrets

Summer Fling

Summer's End

Summer's Wish

Distracted Series

Wake Me

Tame Me

Stand Alone Books

Twisted Rock

Hope Harbor

Raven Falls

For a complete list of books:

http://JillSanders.com

ABOUT THE AUTHOR

Jill Sanders is a New York Times, USA Today, and international best-selling author of Sweet Contemporary Romance, Romantic Suspense, Western Romance, and Paranormal Romance novels. With over 70 books in eleven series, translations into several different languages, and audiobooks there's plenty to choose from. Look for Jill's bestselling stories wherever romance books are sold or visit her at jillsanders.com

Jill comes from a large family with six siblings, including an identical twin. She was raised in the Pacific Northwest and later relocated to Colorado for college and a successful IT career before discovering her talent for writing sweet and sexy page-turners. After Colorado, she decided to move south, living in Texas and now making her home along the Emerald Coast of Florida. You will find that the settings of several of her series are inspired by her time spent living in these areas. She has two sons and off-set the testosterone in her house by adopting three furry little ladies that provide her company while she's locked in her writing cave. She enjoys heading to the beach, hiking, swimming, wine-tasting, and pickle-ball with her husband, and of course writing. If you have read any of her books, you may also notice that there is a love of food, espe-

cially sweets! She has been blamed for a few added pounds by her assistant, editor, and fans... donuts or pie anyone?

Join Jill's Newsletter and get book and sales updates monthly. https://jillsanders.com/newsletter.html

facebook.com/JillSandersBooks

twitter.com/JillMSanders

amazon.com/Jill-Sanders/e/B009M2NFD6?tag=jillmcom-20

bookbub.com/authors/jill-sanders

instagram.com/jillsandersauthor